THE GOA SAGA

GONE

GOA

GONE

BY

EISHA SARKAR

THE WRITE CREED

ISBN: 9781684877928

Published by Eisha Sarkar of The Write Creed in 2021
Cover design by Eisha Sarkar and Joy Fernandes

To Ronit and Rachit

"Even though I walk

through the darkest valley,

I will fear no evil,

for you are with me"

PSALM 23

Dramatis Personae

The Khans:

Aeram Khan: Indian filmstar originally named Aeram Ryan Albuquerque

Farah Khan: Aeram's mother

Sanam Khan: Aeram's sister

Ibrahim Khan: Aeram's stepfather

The Singhs:

Saysha Singh: Aeram's wife

Major General Karanjit Singh: Saysha's father

Shibani Singh: Saysha's stepmother

Vikram Singh: Saysha's stepbrother

The Albuquerques:

Richard Albuquerque: Aeram's father (deceased)

James Albuquerque: Aeram's stunt-double

Daniel Albuquerque aka Danny: Richard's older cousin

Francis Albuquerque: Richard's father

Afonso de Albuquerque: Portuguese conquistador of Goa and Duke of Goa (1453-1515)

The Lebedinskys:

Tatiana Lebedinsky: Saysha's birth-mother (deceased)

Svetlana Lebedinsky: Tatiana's sister

Alexandre Lebedinsky: Tatiana and Svetlana's older brother, Russian mining tycoon

Igor Lebedinsky: Alexandre's only son

Others:

Marea Williams: Richard Albuquerque's housekeeper

Rachel Coutinho: Saysha's friend

Lt General John Coutinho: Rachel's father

Shan: Bollywood's top film director

Imran Bandukwala: Aeram's best friend and film director

Zarine Bandukwala: Aeram's Public Relations manager and Imran's sister

"I knew everything about the men I loved

until the moment they revealed themselves."

SAYSHA

Part 1

GOA

Chapter 1

James and I were sitting in a tiny fishing boat on the Mandovi river. James was rowing and pointed to some mangroves at the far end of the river's bend. I got up to take a look, but typical of me, put one foot wrong, and the boat capsized. We both fell into the water in the middle of the river. The current was strong and carried me away. James swam against it and pulled me towards him. He held me tight and struggled his way to the bank. Just before he was going to pull me out, a reed wrapped around my leg and I went under. He grabbed me by my arm and pulled me up but the reed had its hold too. He didn't give up and with a herculean effort he pulled me onto a rock. I collapsed out of consciousness for some time. Then I felt his lips on mine. It wasn't a kiss, just mouth-to-mouth resuscitation. I kissed him. He stopped. I tried to kiss him again. He sat upright. He frowned and told me, "Don't do that Saysha. I've just got him back. I can't bear to lose either of you." I jolted upright. It was a dream, my first about James. I turned around to see Aeram. He was fast asleep. I kissed him on his lips. Groggily, he kissed me back. I ran my tongue down his torso. He turned over and gave me sex.

I couldn't sleep. It was 4.30 am. I slipped out of the bed, wore Aeram's white shirt from the previous night and stepped into the balcony. It was still dark and the moon shone bright. I looked down to see James cleaning the Bullet parked in the driveway. He was not wearing a shirt. Each rip on his torso glistened in the moonlight. He was gorgeous. He looked up at me. Then he smiled. I returned it. He beckoned me to come downstairs. I hesitated. This wasn't an authorized move. "Come on," he mouthed the words without making a sound. I changed into a white tank top and blue denim shorts and went downstairs to join him. He had put on a thin white *ganji* over his black soccer shorts. He took my hand and led me to the Bullet and asked me to sit. Again, I hesitated. He hadn't taken Aeram's permission. "Come on," he whispered and pulled me towards it. Then he strapped my helmet and helped me onto the bike. I lightly put my hand on his shoulder. He laughed and shook his head. He took my arms and wrapped them around him. I could feel his beating heart and the warmth of his body. Then he whipped out his phone and texted Aeram: "Going to fill the Bullet's tank. Saysha is with me."

I knew Aeram would flip when he read the message. I nervously bit my lip. As James drove faster, my hold on him became tighter and I buried my chin into his shoulder. He threw his head back a bit to look at me and smiled. His lips almost brushed my cheek. We reached the petrol pump. There were a few people. No one recognized us. There were no fans or flashbulbs. James filled up the tank and then we stopped near the river as dawn broke. It was spectacular. In a field nearby, I watched a man climb the coconut tree to pick the fruit. James waited for him to come down and then paid for three. We sipped our coconut water while watching the sun rise over the Mandovi. Then we went back to the villa with a coconut for Aeram and found him still in bed. James made coffee and we sipped it on the porch in silence. We must have spoken five or six words during the forty-five minutes we were alone. This was our first outing without permission, without Aeram's authorization. We had loved it, being in each other's company, without having to explain why and for what. This slowly became a pattern, then a habit and then a reason to exist.

Chapter 2

When Aeram had gifted James the property, I had assumed that from the next time onwards, we would be staying in our house in Bardez. But James would have none of it. We stayed with him at Albuquerque, near Old Goa. He moved to the ground floor guest bedroom from his old house at the edge of the orchard but he still spent some days there. It felt as if we still owned the property. Nothing changed. James was still the driver and stunt-double and my constant companion. Aeram, though sometimes he would still get worked up about James and my friendship, had become a little less controlling as we neared our first wedding anniversary.

I watched Aeram ride pillion with James on the Bullet. That would keep him from getting mobbed by fans. Whenever we took the car out, a black BMW, people stared at us at traffic signals. The helmets and the Bullet camouflaged our celebrity status. Still, because the two of them were so handsome, they did catch people's eyes.

They were gone a long time so I soaked myself in the bath. I lit some candles, sipped wine and threw in a lavender-scented bath bomb. Then I read Neruda's sonnet aloud,

"I want to eat the sunbeam flaring in your lovely body,

the sovereign nose of your arrogant face,

I want to eat the fleeting shade of your lashes,"

I had closed my eyes and almost dozed off when I heard the door open. Aeram peeked into the bathroom. He eyed me with lust. I beckoned him to come sit with me. He undressed in seconds and slowly entered the bath.

"My beautiful, Saysha," he said, and kissed me on my neck. We made love in the bath and sat in the tub exhausted and entwined.

In the afternoon, I sat at the dining table working on James's sketch. The sun streamed in through the rattan blinds on the windows and cast a pattern of shadows on his gorgeous body. This time, I worked on his left eye. I remembered our last conversation when we had sat like this. How intense it was; how he had made me feel, without even touching me. It still gave me goosebumps. This time, we sat in silence till we heard footsteps. It was Aeram. He walked up to us and when he saw the drawing he froze. He looked at James who sat expressionless. Then he looked at me. I bit my lip but thankfully it did not bleed this time. I could see his jaw tighten. James got up and said, "I'll leave."

"No," I shouted and held his hand tight. Aeram's eyes moved to our hands. James raised an eyebrow.

"Sit," I ordered.

Aeram looked at me incredulously. He turned red. James watched us, shook his head and sat down in his chair. His head was lowered but I could see his lips were curving very slightly into a smile.

Then I turned to Aeram and told him, "This is my project. James will leave when I am done." I left James's hand and held Aeram's. "Come, sit next to me and watch me draw." He started to open his mouth to say something but then he stopped and quietly pulled the chair next to me.

I began to sketch again.

After five minutes, I heard a chuckle. It was Aeram. "You know, I love you, Saysha," he said, stroking my head. "I love you too, Aeram," I told him without looking up. James watched us quietly. "But, when you boss over me like this, I go crazy about you," Aeram laughed. I stopped drawing and turned towards him. The man was insane. "Seriously," he said and laughed again. I did not know what to make of it so I smiled. He held my hand and looked into my eyes, "I like it when you put me in place."

I smiled and gave him a peck on the cheek.

James smiled.

Aeram glared at him and shouted, "Hey, lose that smirk."

James laughed out loud. He threw his head back. I giggled. Aeram shook his head, "The two of you drive me insane."

"Hey, can you please sit still?" I admonished James. He sat upright but continued to smile.

Aeram asked him, "Want some *feni?*"

James nodded. Aeram rose to get a bottle from the bar in the corner of the living room. I smiled at James. He blew me a kiss. I blushed.

Aeram poured us each a glass and then raised a toast, "To Saysha."

Then Aeram moved towards the old gramophone next to the liquor cabinet and pulled out a vinyl from a leather-covered Louis Vuitton travel chest from under the table where the gramophone was. "I haven't seen anyone play a gramophone in my life!" My voice came out squeaky. James laughed. The room filled with the voice of Engelbert Humperdinck crooning *Can't Take My Eyes Off You.* James rolled his eyes and muttered under his breath, "Sweet Jesus!" He guzzled the *feni*, kicked his chair backwards, got up and left. Aeram smirked and walked towards me. He bent down to kiss my cheek and glanced at the door from which James had left and chuckled, "That didn't take long."

Chapter 3

We invited Rachel from Mumbai to stay with us for a few days. Lionel would join us at the end of the week. I was looking forward to having someone else in the house besides Aeram and James. When she burst in through the door, she was full of awe. James, who had picked her from the airport, put her bags in the spare bedroom upstairs because he was staying in the guest room on the ground floor. I took Rachel on a tour of the villa and then we sat on the balcony looking over the orchard. Aeram was away shooting a commercial at Calangute beach.

James walked in, shirtless, wearing only his low-slung ripped blue jeans. He smiled at Rachel, who was ogling at him, then turned towards me and said, "Saysha, if you need anything, call me. I'll be in the garage. Will join you for lunch." I nodded. "Thanks, James." He smiled and left us.

Rachel let out a sigh. "Why is he gay?" I blushed. "He is so bloody hot, Saysha! How lucky you are, hanging out with two gorgeous men all the time, while the rest of us have to just make do with the ordinary."

I laughed. "Well, Lionel is quite good looking too."

"But not like this," she pointed at the door, from which James had exited moments ago. "Why the hell is he gay? He could get any woman in bed."

"Well, he has slept with many women," I offered. Rachel's mouth opened. "You had a conversation about that with him? Isn't he your driver?"

I turned a deep red. "He's also our friend." I couldn't tell her he was Aeram's brother. Between the three of us, we had decided we would not tell anyone that, not even Sanam, not until Aeram and James were ready to go public with it."

Rachel looked at me incredulously. "Who makes friends with their drivers? You guys should hang out with people of your status and kind." I should have retorted that she was merely a pastry chef talking to a superstar's wife and had no business to make a comment like that but I kept my mouth shut.

Thankfully, Aeram walked in right then. "Hi Rachel," he said in his sexy voice. "Hi Aeram," she said in her singsong voice. She put her arms around his neck and planted a kiss on his cheek. I looked away. After almost a year, I still hadn't got used to women hugging and kissing him as if he belonged to them. Sometimes, I wished I was as possessive of him as he was of me but his public persona was such that it would be difficult to keep people at bay. Aeram walked towards me, took me in his arms and lightly kissed my lips. "How is my wife?" I smiled in response.

Then James walked in with Candy, our maid-cum-cook, and laid out a buffet for lunch: pork vindaloo, prawn curry, fried pomfret, chicken cafreal, *pav* and heaps of rice.

"You guys eat so much every day?" Rachel asked between spoonfuls of vindaloo and rice. "No, this is for you," I told her. She rolled her eyes. I watched James, who was mopping up vindaloo with *pav*. He had put on a see-through vest. He saw me watching him, then put his plate aside and walked towards me. My heart skipped a beat. I threw a glance at Aeram, who was busy sucking bits of fish from the bone of the pomfret. James brought his lips really close to my ear and whispered, "Come with me after lunch. I'll show you something." I looked at him quizzically. Then I noticed Rachel was watching us closely. I simply nodded.

James then went to sit next to Aeram, who was struggling to debone the fish head. His forehead was furrowed and his jaw was tight. His plate was disgustingly messy. Anyone else would have asked for another plate and another fish but Aeram kept picking at it with vengeance. A bead of sweat trickled down his brow. James watched him for five minutes and then put his hand on Aeram's shoulder. He frowned and shrugged. "What?" James took the plate away from him. Aeram was about to protest but James threw the remnants of the fish into a bin. He took another pomfret and, with a knife and fork, cleaned out the whole fish in minutes and passed it to Aeram. "That's practice," he said, patting his brother's shoulder. Aeram sighed with relief and polished the fish off in seconds. Rachel giggled and teased Aeram, "What *yaar*! You can't even pick the bones off the fish yourself. You're so spoilt." Aeram turned red but didn't look up from his empty plate. He pretended to mop up the remnants of the sauce with his fingers and sucked them one by one. James glared at Rachel but she didn't notice. He turned to Aeram, put his hand on his shoulder and said, "Hey, I am taking the Bullet for a refill after this. Saysha is coming with me." I watched the blood rise in Aeram's cheeks and was going to tell him no, but he just said, "Okay." I was surprised. James winked at me.

From the balcony, Rachel and Aeram watched me get onto the bike behind James. Neither of us wore helmets. I lightly put my hands on his shoulders. He laughed and wrapped them around him. I looked up to see my husband. He waved a goodbye. I started to relax as we joined the traffic on the main road. I rested my chin on his shoulder. He threw his head back, turned it a little and gave me a kiss on my cheek. A shiver ran through my body. We filled the tank at the petrol pump and then he asked me to sit in the front.

"I don't know how to ride, James," I pleaded.

"Come on," he pulled my hand.

I didn't budge. There was no way I was going to be riding the Bullet on the road. Then James did something that changed me forever.

He picked me up and seated me on the bike. I was too shocked to react.

"Kick, hard," he ordered. I tried, the bike whirred and stopped. I tried to get off but his hands pressed down my bare shoulders. Another shiver ran through my body.

"Try again," he ordered. People started to look at us. Some even cheered. I blushed and shook my head.

After several attempts, I managed to kick the bike to a start. James sat behind me. He put his arms around my waist and held me tight. I felt his chin on my shoulder. His lips brushed against my skin. A knot started to form in my stomach. I tried to focus on the road. The Bullet picked up speed and I felt more in control, I felt the wind in my face and the warmth of the body behind me. Then James asked me to take a turn and stop right near the Mandovi. We got off the bike. He climbed upon a rock on the bank, slipped out of his sandals and dipped his feet into the river. I took my loafers off and sat next to him. There was a light breeze. He wrapped me in his arms and we sat like that for a while, just listening to the birds and the water. I rested my head on his chest. After savouring a few more minutes of stillness, he loosened his hold of me and put his forehead to mine. His lips were less than an inch away from mine. In a deep sexy voice he said, "I love you, Saysha, more than anything else in this world. I love your heart; I love your soul. And I will always be there for you, watching you, protecting you." His lips moved to my forehead and planted a kiss there.

I sat behind James as we made our way back to the villa. From the orchard gates, I could see Aeram pacing up and down the porch. James threw his head back and whispered, "It's ok." His lips brushed my cheek. Aeram ran down the steps and helped me off the bike. He then gave me a long kiss on my lips. James looked away. Rachel watched us with curiosity. I knew she had many questions but I had no answers, yet. When we broke after the kiss, I whispered to Aeram, "Let's go for a bath, baby." He grinned and carried me into the house.

As I ran the loofah over his foam-covered body in the bath, I asked him why he had allowed James to take me with him.

Aeram sighed, "Because I have taken too many things away from you; your parents, your education, your friends, your chance to be like any other twenty-three-year-old, your ambitions, your career. I can't give you normal. I am not normal…" He paused, as if he was searching for words.

"…He can. He can take you anywhere, without fans and photographers. He is normal. Most people call him abnormal because he's gay. But look at me, I am straight as a rod, but wired in a way that's not normal. I know he loves you too much to not hurt you and I know he loves me too much to not hurt me. It's a good space to be in."

Aeram was deep, very deep and sometimes, even I couldn't understand how someone as possessive and controlling as him could accept the fact that I had spent an afternoon in the company of another man, his brother. There seemed to be two people within him, one very mature, another child-like, who were always battling each other to come on top. Aeram would need to be reassured again and again that James and I loved each other in a different way. But he never questioned James when he proposed to take me somewhere. James never asked. In James's company, Aeram had started dealing with his control issues with a lot more maturity. James was good for Sanam and me but for Aeram, he was the balm that healed all wounds, the hand that cared, the substitute of the father he never really had.

"You said, you're straight as a rod," I chuckled. He looked at me and grinned. We made love in the tub.

Chapter 4

Rachel and I were walking through the orchards, trying to keep pace with James, who strode without a shirt on his back. His blue jeans hung low, revealing the waistband of his white underwear. When he was out of earshot, Rachel turned to me and scowled. "What exactly did I see?"

I knew what she was getting at but feigned ignorance and started talking about Alphonso mangoes. "Stop it, Saysha," she shouted. "What the hell are the three of you up to?"

I shrugged and asked, "What?"

She put her hands on her hips and demanded an explanation. "Did I just see your driver whisking you out for a ride on the bike and your crazy controlling husband agreeing to it and then pacing up and down the porch as if you were kidnapped or something? The man must have lost more calories than all that he put in his mouth for lunch."

"James is our friend. Not just a driver, Rachel."

She was curious. "Where did he take you?"

"He was teaching me how to ride the Bullet." It wasn't exactly a lie.

She raised her eyebrows. "And how does Aeram even tolerate that?"

I looked down and picked up a *vovlam* flower. James had told me they were very rare. Rachel watched me. "He can't tell much to James. They go back a long way."

She put her hands on her hips again, frowned and asked, "How long?"

"Since childhood. They grew up together in this house," I replied.

Rachel's mouth opened in shock. She asked, "They're related?"

"Yes, through their father."

"Saysha," James hollered, "Come here." Relieved, I picked up the pace.

Rachel shook her head and muttered. "That's the first time I have seen a driver barking commands at a mistress. Never happened in cantonment life!"

I smiled. James showed us different kinds of mushrooms, some poisonous, others not. Rachel raised her eyebrows and asked, "Any hallucinogenic ones here?"

James laughed and shook his head. "No."

We both admired his features in the scattered sunlight that streamed in from between leaves. He looked stunning. He saw me admiring him.

Rachel couldn't resist. She asked him the obvious question. "Why are you gay?"

I was taken aback by her directness.

He walked up to her, looked her in the eye and in his deep sexy voice asked, "Why not?"

For the first time in my life, I found Rachel nervous. "Well... you could have any woman. You're gorgeous."

James threw his head back and laughed. "Really? Well, I am just keeping my options open, then." He turned away from her, looked at me and winked. My cheeks were warming up.

"I think we better head back," I mumbled and turned towards the path leading us out of the orchard to the house. James and Rachel followed a few paces behind me. They were giggling about something. Rachel was flirting with him, I gathered from her singsong voice, and he was enjoying it. A weird feeling of jealousy took over. As soon as I reached the villa, I ran straight into Aeram's waiting arms and kissed him hard and long. When we broke off, I glanced at James. He looked away.

Chapter 5

We were buttering toast for breakfast when James walked in and sat next to Rachel. He wore only his soccer shorts. Rachel eyed him with lust. "What's the plan for the day?" She was asking me but staring at him.

"We're thinking of going to the Sinquerium beach at the Taj later, maybe even the pool there," I told her and glared at James. His jaw tightened. He cut a piece of the omelette on his plate, put it in his mouth with the fork and chewed it very, very slowly.

"Great!" Rachel exclaimed and then turned to my husband. "Aeram, this place is heaven. But it's missing a pool. You've got to make one here."

I was about to say something when Aeram put his hand on mine. "Well, ask him," he said, pointing to James, "It's his house and land, not mine." Rachel's jaw dropped. James rolled his eyes and said, "Oh come on, if you want a pool, you'll have a pool."

Rachel was speechless. James asked me. "Saysha, do you want a pool here?" I avoided eye contact and shook my head. He smiled. His trees were safe. He did not want to clear any part of the land he had been planting since his early childhood for a swimming pool.

We watched Aeram and James hop onto the Bullet for a ride to Panjim. Rachel and I were alone.

She crossed her arms. "He owns this whole thing, like every piece of it?"

I nodded.

"Then why the hell is he a driver and stunt-double?"

"Because he wants to be and Aeram trusts only him," I replied, unconvincingly.

She shook her head. "I think James likes you." Her eyes searched my face for a clue.

"What? He's gay!"

She said, "You told me he has slept with women before."

"Yes…"

She held my hand, "I think he wants you."

This was too much for me to process. James had told me he loved me and I loved him but we knew there couldn't be any sex involved.

"He looks at you like a man in love looks at a woman, Saysha. A man who is madly in love. He probably loves you as much as Aeram does, if not more."

I gulped.

She raised her eyebrows, "Why was he working as an extra if he owned all of this?"

I had to tell her. "He didn't. Aeram just gifted him this whole property two months ago."

She covered her mouth with her hands. "What!! Are you serious?"

I nodded silently.

"Who does that? Is he insane?" She was shouting.

"He is," I confirmed. There was something seriously wrong with my husband.

She rolled her eyes and asked, "Like gifted? Free?"

I nodded in affirmation.

She demanded, "Why?"

I shrugged.

She quipped, "Well Saysha, if he ever thinks of gifting any other villas, houses, flats, farms or orchards, please remind him of me."

I laughed out loud.

"Hey girls," Aeram called out. He carried a crate of beer. James, behind him, had his arms wrapped around packages of foods: fried fish, Goan sausages, *pav* and all kinds of chips.

Rachel asked Aeram, "How do you maintain a body like that while eating all this junk?"

He laughed. "I told you, Saysha keeps me on my toes. Spend two weeks with her and she'll give you enough reason to worry about her and lose weight." I rolled my eyes. James chuckled. I opened my mouth to say something but Aeram continued, "Besides, I don't eat like this 365 days a year. Only, when I am here."

"The bigger headache was carrying all of this on the Bullet, that crate especially," James chuckled. When he didn't see me smile, he raised his eyebrows. I turned away.

The next day, Lionel joined us and we spent the day touring: Anjuna, Chapora and Candolim. Lionel was a man of the sea and he loved gadgets, cars and bikes. The men huddled together while Rachel and I did loads of shopping.

I watched Rachel and Lionel when they were together. They seemed like they were in love but they were both so independent that they didn't live for each other. They seemed content in their own spaces. It wasn't anything like I had known in love, because the two men I loved, loved me with an intensity that was extraordinary.

The morning they were leaving, outside the airport, Rachel hugged us all, even James. She whispered something in his ear that made him smile and there was a glint in his eye.

Half hour later, she texted me as soon as she boarded the flight:

Rachel: Had a lovely time Saysha. Thank you for everything. You're a lucky girl to have two people who are so crazy about you. See you in Mumbai, love.

James looked at me in the rear-view mirror. Our eyes met briefly. His forehead furrowed. I lay my head on Aeram's chest as we drove in through the large white gates of the plantation.

Chapter 6

James sat opposite me while I scratched the paper with the graphite to sketch his lips. A single ray of sunlight cut diagonally across them. He had a scar from the cut that Aeram had delivered by punching him for kissing him in his sleep. Aeram had to go to Panjim to complete some paperwork for the transfer of the property to James. After sitting still for a long time, he asked softly, "Saysha, what's on your mind?"

I looked up and bit my lip.

"Please tell me," James pressed my hand. I shivered. He withdrew. He moved to the chair next to me. I did not look at him. He took the graphite from my hand and put it down on the table. "Saysha," James whispered, turning my face towards him and cupping it with both hands, "Please tell me. You haven't been the same since we walked the orchard with Rachel. What is on your mind, darling?"

The word, 'darling', was too much. A tear trickled down my cheek. "Saysha, please don't," he said and wiped it away with his thumb. "What is the matter?" He brought his lips very close to mine. I could feel his warm breath as he uttered those words, "Saysha, I love you more than anything else in the world. You are the reason for my existence. I cannot bear to see you cry like this."

I bit my lip so hard that it bled. "Saysha," James whispered, and then gently kissed my lower lip. Then he got up to go to the guest bedroom. He came back with a handkerchief and a glass of water. Dabbing my lip, he asked, "Why are you so stressed?"

Finally, my tongue found the words, "Because you love me like a man loves a woman."

He looked at me and held my hand, "Yes."

"But you're gay." I shouted more out of shock than reproach.

He stroked my cheek and said, "I have been since I was fifteen and have never felt this way for any woman before. I tried talking myself out of it, avoided being your friend, hardly spoke to you but now I can't keep myself away from you. I don't know what it means. But I will never hurt you or him because of how I feel for you."

I kissed him. And he kissed me back. It was a long, deep kiss. I kept kissing him again and again while my hand reached deep into his shirt and caressed his smooth chest. Tia had told me what a fantastic kisser he was. It was an understatement. I never thought anyone could be better than Aeram but James proved me wrong in every way. When we broke off, he put his forehead against mine and sighed. "I love you, Saysha." He then gave me a peck on my cheek, got up and left.

When Aeram came back late in the evening, I fixed his bath. "Join me, Saysha. Please." I unrobed and sat next to him. He nibbled at my earlobe and wrapped his arms around me. Guilt rose in my heart. I did not know what to tell him. My heart was beating fast. He put his lips next to my ear. "Saysha, why did you kiss him?" I sat upright and turned to him. "I'm so sorry, Aeram… I just…" Tears rolled down my cheeks. He was crying too. "I love you too much to let go of you, Saysha. I can't live without you." I kissed him on his lips. He didn't kiss me back. "Please, please never do that again. Please." He was begging me. I promised. Then he kissed me long and deep. We made love in the tub and then in bed. As I lay awake in his arms, I thought about James and Aeram.

"What are you thinking?" Aeram was awake.

"About you and James."

"Well, we're now a threesome, aren't we?" He chuckled.

I looked away.

He took my hand in his.

"The problem is, Saysha, it's very easy to fall in love with you. And I can't be mad at anyone for doing that. It's the way you are. You deserve to be loved. You want to be loved. You need to be loved." I kissed him on his cheek. He continued, "But, having said that, I can't share you with anyone. So tomorrow, you'll be leaving for Delhi. I have spoken with your father. Neelam has had to camp in Delhi to research stuff for the period movie Shweta has just bagged. You'll be working on it. I'll join you next week. I need to sort things regarding the property here with James. Something big is coming and we need to be ready."

He had planned everything without even asking me once. All I could do was nod in agreement because I was the guilty party. Then I asked, "And James?"

Aeram sighed, "He has to be here for a while. He'll join us in Mumbai after a month. Hopefully, things here will be settled by then."

I sighed. He stroked my head and said, "It's good to keep a little distance, Saysha. He's confused because he has always been gay. And you've never known any guy other than me. I know you love him and he loves you. But I love you both a bit too much to lose either of you. Please don't make it more complicated than it already is."

I caressed his chest.

"Can I… umm… tell him goodbye?"

He kissed me on my cheek and said, "Of course!"

Since Aeram had a photo shoot for a magazine at Calangute, it was James who dropped me at the airport. I sat next to him in the front, looking out of the window, as we drove in silence. We reached the airport and he put my bags in a trolley. I was trying to think of something to say, when he wrapped his arms around me tightly and planted a kiss on my forehead. "I'll miss you, Saysha. Take care," he whispered and let me go.

PART 2

NEW DELHI

Chapter 7

"There you are, young lady," John Uncle's baritone made me turn right round. He had come from Shimla for the weekend and was catching up with Dad over a few glasses of scotch. Rachel's father had known me since I was a toddler. "Come here, darling," he beckoned and I gave him a hug. "Rachel loved your villa and orchards in Old Goa. Karanjit and I want to visit too, now."

"Sure, Uncle," I smiled at him.

"Yes, I have never been there. Though Richard had asked all the boys at school to come home once but I was down with malaria one year and the next year with typhoid so I missed it. It used to be the event of the year in those days."

This came as a surprise.

My heart was racing, but I tried to keep my voice as normal as was possible to ask, "Uncle, you knew Richard Albuquerque?"

"Yes, for a few years, he was at our boarding school in Mapusa. Then they sent him to Doon or Sherwood, I think."

I asked, "How was he?"

"Well, he was quite a mild person. Used to paint, plant, fish, read and play soccer. Never fought with anyone. Some called him 'soft'. He was always on his own. But once a year, his mother ensured that all the boys in his class were treated to the mangoes from the orchards at Albuquerque."

I smiled.

"Does Danny still live around there?" He asked.

I frowned. "Who?"

"Richard's cousin, Daniel Albuquerque. He was a couple of years older, a complete bully. They used to live in the same house till Richard was twenty-one or something. Danny had acted funny with the housekeeper's daughter, apparently. Then he got kicked out and was told never to come back. I think he rented a house down the road some years ago. Anyway, this was ages ago. Saysha, are you okay?"

I was too shocked to react. The housekeeper's daughter was Marea, Aeram and James's mother. Dad cleared his throat. It brought me back to the present.

My longing for Aeram's smell, his breath on my body, his taste, his touch kept me awake that night. At two in the morning, I texted him:

Saysha: Hi

Aeram: Hi

Saysha: I miss you

Aeram: I miss you too much. Just five more days, baby

Saysha: John Uncle came over today. Rachel's Dad

Aeram: Ok

Saysha: He knew Richard and then mentioned someone by the name of Daniel Albuquerque. I told him I didn't know

There was no response.

Saysha: You there?

Aeram: I love you Saysha. I'll be in your arms soon. Goodnight.

I couldn't sleep. Aeram had changed the topic. I texted James.

Saysha: Hi

After what seemed like minutes but was only a few seconds, there was a response.

James: Hi Saysha

Saysha: I miss you James

There was no answer

After minutes, I wrote again,

Saysha: You there?

James: Saysha, are you trying to ask me a question Aeram doesn't want to answer?

Damn! They told each other everything and yet feigned as if they hardly talked.

Saysha: Yes James. Do you know Richard's cousin Daniel Albuquerque?

James: Yes. And that is what is keeping you so far away from the two of us. Stay happy in Delhi, Saysha. We'll talk when we meet.

I realized that Aeram didn't send me to Delhi to punish me for kissing James. "Something big is coming…" were his words. Daniel Albuquerque? I googled him. His Facebook and LinkedIn pages were private but there were some articles on Goan websites that mentioned his name. I scrolled through them. He had been invited as chief guest to a school function, another was about a store opening where there was a picture of a crowd in front of a store but no captions and there was a quote from him in an article about the upcoming elections in Goa where he said, "Goa must shed its colonial history. I am ashamed to be an Albuquerque. All those who bear that name should also be ashamed and give up their huge estates and properties to the state or the church." This hit me like a thunderbolt. I looked for his picture. There were none made available to the public.

Chapter 8

Neelam had camped in a tiny office in a building full of newspaper offices at Bahadur Shah Zafar Road. While it helped her access the media and their archives for her research, it posed a problem for me. Aeram and James had strived very hard to keep me away from the media and working in an office full of newspaper journalists was the last thing they wanted, especially now, when neither of them were in Delhi to protect me. Neelam came up with the solution. I was to work from home. Every morning, she would send me emails about the kind of concepts and moods Shweta was looking to translate on screen and I had to burrow into the internet to find references. Which, to put into simpler words, she asked me to watch all kinds of period films, frame-by-frame, and make notes on sets, props, costumes, colours, lights, outdoor and indoor set design, etc.

I never knew there could be a job in the world where you would just have to watch films and TV all day and get paid for it, till I actually started working in the film industry.

On the first day, I watched *Mughal-e-Azam*, *Pakeezah* and *Jodhaa Akbar*. Initially, I loved the idea of the binge. But watching a movie frame by frame and taking notes was a very different experience. A three-hour movie took me five to process and by the end of the day, my neck was so stiff that only Aeram's firm hand could remove the knots. I missed him. Delhi brought back memories of our college, our dates and the night we waltzed to Neruda in my room, a life we had shared before James had walked into it and changed both of us, forever. Aeram had told me a bit of distance would help and I could see why. It took me a while, but I finally reconciled to the fact that as much as I loved James and he loved me, it could not compare with the love I had for Aeram. I had lost the man and got him back and there was no way I wanted to lose him again. Yes, I loved James, but that love would have to be different, shown differently and felt differently. I had always thought Aeram to be immature because of his possessiveness but the way he managed James and me in that situation spoke of his deep insight into our emotions and souls. Not many men had the courage to do that. But Aeram was not normal. He was extraordinary.

I was tossing and turning in bed unable to sleep when he texted.

Aeram: Hey baby

Saysha: Hi darling. I miss you so much. I want you NOW!

Aeram: Then open the window

Saysha: What?

I got out of bed and walked towards the window. He was waving at me from the lawn. I slid the window open. He took a few steps back and then made the leap. I pulled his heavy frame in and he fell on top of me on the floor. We made love right there and fell off to sleep on the floor.

The next morning, I felt his stubble on my cheek. Aeram had always been very particular about grooming. He looked handsome in a rugged sort of way. I caressed his cheek. He turned over and kissed me.

I asked him, "You were going to arrive the day after. How are you here today?"

"I had to avoid the press so PR leaked the date for the day after while I flew economy today," he whispered and nibbled my earlobe.

"I have missed you like crazy, Aeram."

He didn't reply. He moved his lips and tongue hungrily all over me.

As we lay in each other's arms post-coitus, I asked him the question that had been in my head for the last few days: "Is Daniel Albuquerque after the villa?"

Aeram looked at me and sighed, "Yes."

I turned towards him. Our lips were almost touching. "But you own it, right, as the legal heir and you've renovated it too, right?"

He stroked my cheek and whispered, "Yes, I have but he's still fighting for it."

This was discomforting. I loved the estate. "Why? On what basis?"

Aeram caressed my bare back and replied, "On the basis that he is the only true Albuquerque. Not me."

"How? Richard left it to you, right?"

He laughed. "Actually... no... Richard left it to the 'true male heir' of the Albuquerque clan."

I frowned. "That is so cryptic. Why?"

"There is a clause," he said slowly, "that Manuel's grandson, Xavier Albuquerque, had put in at the time of the Inquisition in Goa in the sixteenth century. They did not want to 'contaminate' their line with non-Christian blood so they married pure Portuguese and ensured that all the successors to the estate were Catholics. Then Richard married my mother,

Farah, after his initial hesitation. Though Sanam and I were not born to her, we are her legal children. My last name is Khan, not Albuquerque. Even if I revert to my birth-name, which I don't want to, I cannot be the legal heir because everyone knows I am half-Muslim. I practise Islam privately. And so does Sanam. I think Papa knew there would be a complication there so he made a second will that he left with Ammi and that was to be disclosed only on Ammi's death. Ammi had been working on Albuquerque's disputes since she was an intern. He knew she would be able to give James what he rightly deserved. I don't think Papa ever imagined the circumstances where James would be forced out of our lives for fifteen years and Ammi would die just months after my twenty-first birthday. Unlike his previous will, in his second one, he named his true and only legal heir, his only Catholic son, who was born of an illegitimate affair but who looks exactly like him so there's no mistaking he is Richard's son, his eldest, James Christian Albuquerque."

My jaw dropped. "What? I thought you just gifted him the estate."

Aeram shook his head. "It wasn't mine in the first place. He owns them all: Old Goa, Mapusa and Bardez as well as a ranch Richard owned at Albuquerque, New Mexico, in the US, a house in Alhandra and two hotels in Lisbon in Portugal. In fact, he gifted Bardez to us."

What the...

"The fact that James is illegitimate... does that matter?" I still couldn't believe he owned everything.

Aeram chuckled. "Well, Afonso Albuquerque's heir, Brás, was born out of an illegitimate affair. Manuel, the Goan ancestor of the Albuquerque line was born out of wedlock. Illegitimacy is not the problem. You would rather be illegitimate and Catholic than legitimate and Muslim."

Then he became serious again. "My mother, Farah, wrote Sanam and me out of Richard's will by marrying my stepfather, Ibrahim Khan. She had her reasons. Delhi wasn't the best place for a young single woman with two little children. She sought the safety and protection of a name. She wanted us to have a father-like figure. Ibrahim was her older cousin. The age difference between Ammi and him was nineteen years. He had been a widower for five years and his only son, Feroz, was ten years older than me. He was seventeen and I was seven when Ammi married Ibrahim. Feroz left for the US to study after he turned eighteen. I... never liked him."

His mouth quivered when he mentioned Feroz's name but he recovered quickly.

There were so many questions racing through my head. "Is that why you went looking for James?"

He kissed me on my forehead. "I missed you like crazy when you left for Shimla. You had changed your number and email id. I couldn't even call you. I begged your father to tell me where you were but he didn't say anything. I contemplated suicide."

What? I never realized how deep his love for me was. I cupped his face in my hands and whispered, "No! Please, no!" Aeram looked me in the eye, a tear rolled down his cheek, "You know I am weird and insane, Saysha. I can do anything for you. And I can do anything if I lose you."

"No, you won't. You are not going to even think about that," I admonished him.

He laughed, "I go crazy about you when you boss over me." He kissed me.

When we broke away, he continued the story. "When Ammi was diagnosed with cancer and we discovered it was terminal, I suggested to her that we move to Mumbai for treatment at

Tata Hospital. We had got the news of her diagnosis on the day I had invited you to our house for dinner. The last day we met before you left me. I was really depressed with her diagnosis and with you leaving me like that so I wanted to just get out of Delhi. I told Ammi that I would be meeting some doctors at Tata. That's when she told me about James and both Papa's wills. She had tried to track him down with the help of the cops she knew and had figured he was a model in Mumbai. She didn't know his whereabouts but had managed to find a picture in an ad in a magazine. When I randomly joked with Imran that I might have found my doppelgänger and showed him the photo, Imran suggested we use him as my stunt-double in *Sherlock Gomes*. He had just convinced Amazon to produce the series and was keen to go to Mumbai to get started. Imran used his contacts in the film industry and found James. The moment I walked into his apartment and said my name he knew who I was and why I was there. We talked about everything. I spent the whole evening. You've seen his home and you know my OCD about tiny places. But I didn't care. He made the most awesome coffee ever and I sat my butt down and chatted with him. I told him about everything, all those years we had missed being with each other, about school, college, Delhi, theatre and you. I talked and talked and he just listened."

He must have seen the puzzled look on my face. Aeram wasn't much of a talker. I had known him for four years but he had never opened his heart and talked to me about everything. I had to ask him questions that he would answer according to his level of comfort. If he wasn't comfortable, he would simply shrug or laugh it off.

"I have never felt that connection with anyone else, Saysha. Not even you. He's like oxygen to me. I cannot live without him. I went back to Delhi after a week and told Ammi everything. She was very happy. The only thing I did not know at that point of time was that he was not my half-brother, but my real brother. Ammi had saved that bit of news till moments before her death and to prevent me from doing anything rash like contemplating suicide, she had legally made me the custodian of Papa's wills till I could put James in the place he deserves to be. I am my mother's son, Saysha."

"She must be very proud of you, Aeram," I told him, while patting his cheek. Two dimples formed.

Chapter 9

Since Aeram had a couple of public engagements, including a store's inauguration at one of Gurgaon's swanky malls, I busied myself with research on period films. I noticed how the same props were used in many films shot over a particular period; the lamps, chandeliers, candelabras, furniture, curtains, painted backdrops, posters, beaded garlands, tapestry, carpets, water fountains, sculptures, etc. I made a list of items that could be reused in the new film. Once the screenplay was finalized and Shweta had her copy, she would sit with the director and the cameraman to break up each individual scene frame by frame to design the set for a particular mood. Till then, we were just building up lists, catalogues, references and some inventory. When I was not busy with that, I sketched Vikram, my younger brother who would finish school the next year and join the army or the air force. He was becoming taller and handsome. He might have had a girlfriend but there was no way I was going to ask him that.

I was hoping to meet Sanam in Delhi, but my trip had been planned so suddenly that I hadn't had the time to call her until after I landed in New Delhi and then discovered that she had gone to Manali with her friends for a week of relaxation.

After a hectic day of press conferences, photo-shoots and ribbon-cutting engagements, Aeram returned home. Vikram was sitting opposite me at the dining table and I was sketching his right eye. Aeram kissed me on my cheek and looked at the sketch. He smiled. Then he asked me, "Saysha, can you get the bathwater ready for me, please?"

Vikram raised an eyebrow while Aeram made his way to my bedroom. "*Didi*, don't tell me Mr Superstar doesn't know how to mix hot and cold water."

I laughed and got up from my chair. His eyes followed me to the bedroom.

No sooner had I closed the door than Aeram grabbed me from behind and dragged me into the bed. "I have missed you like crazy today, Saysha," he said, running his hands over my breasts and unbuttoning my top. We made love on the bed and then again in the shower. My tiny bathroom could not accommodate a bathtub.

That night, I thought of Daniel Albuquerque again. I had forgotten to ask Aeram about him and now he was fast asleep. I googled the man. This time there were many news articles about him, with his picture. He was chubby, with ruddy cheeks, brown eyes like Aeram's, a slight grey stubble and salt-and-pepper hair. The most commonly used picture was of him looking very drunk with his arm around a waif-thin blonde woman barely out of her teens who was spilling out of her tight red cleavage-baring mini-dress. John Uncle had called him a bully. It wasn't the face of an honest man. I clicked on the *Panjim Pioneer's* headline, "Daniel Albuquerque dies in car crash." The story followed:

Panjim: Goa's evergreen party-hopper Daniel Albuquerque aka Danny died in a car crash late Friday evening on his way back to Albuquerque near Old Goa from Panjim.

Post-mortem reports suggest that Albuquerque was driving under the influence of alcohol and cocaine. His Hyundai Verna crashed into a black BMW just as they were about to enter the Ponte de Linhares Causeway. The name of the driver of the BMW has been withheld on his request. He has sustained major injuries but is now stable.

Sixty-nine-year-old Albuquerque belonged to an old Portuguese family who have estates in Old Goa, Mapusa and Bardez. Before the crash, Albuquerque had met with his lawyer in Panjim regarding matters related to those estates. He was hoping to contest the next elections on the Nationalist Party ticket.

Albuquerque had earlier said he wanted to shed his linkage to Goa's colonial past and preferred to be addressed only as Danny.

PART 3
PARIS

Chapter 10

Three weeks before our first wedding anniversary, we finally went on our honeymoon. Most people would count Shimla and Goa as honeymoon destinations but we couldn't because James was always with us. When Aeram told me that we would not be going to Mumbai from Delhi but to Paris for our honeymoon, I almost collapsed with excitement. Paris meant I needed to shop and thankfully Sanam was back from her sojourn in the hills to help me with that on my last day in Delhi. September was going to be cold in Europe so we bought coats, scarves and gloves of every type. I bought designer dresses, gowns that were fit for the red carpet, Christian Louboutin heels that I could barely stand in but had to wear because they were a gift from Sanam, skinny jeans, white sneakers and jackets of varying lengths and makes. I also had to buy a bag, a Louis Vuitton. My husband was proud.

We flew first class in Air France. The waiter brought us two glasses of champagne with strawberries. It was going to be a good flight. Aeram had booked the entire row, that is, both the cabins on either side of the aisle, to give us complete privacy. Unlike most actors and filmmakers, my husband was such a private person that he never took his staff with him even during his foreign schedules, with the exception of James and sometimes, Zarine, who managed his public relations. If he needed people, he hired them locally. Basically, there would be no one to interrupt us during our nine-hour lovemaking and merrymaking session in the sky. No sooner had the flight taken off, we drew the curtains and sank into each other. It was like those corner seats in the cinema hall.

The smell of perfume announced to us that we were in Charles de Gaulle Airport in Paris. On our way out of the Arrivals, I couldn't help stopping at a pretty bakery that was selling macaroons of all colours. We both picked one each, a coffee and a raspberry, and tasted heaven.

Aeram had booked a huge three-bedroom apartment close to Pont de l'Alma which gave us an unobstructed view of the River Seine and the Eiffel Tower. He collected the keys from the caretaker, Victor, and carried me up two flights of stairs in his arms instead of taking the elevator, with the keys dangling in his mouth. He asked me to unlock the door without putting me down and when I did, he took me straight to the bedroom. We made out before our bags made their way up.

After we had showered and dressed ourselves in casuals, we took a walk along the river. It was chilly so we wore our coats and huddled together to keep warm. And we finally French-kissed in France with the Eiffel Tower in the distance.

The fortnight went by in a jiffy. We visited the Louvre, Hotel de Ville, Musée Rodin, the weird-looking Centre Pompidou, Arc de Triomphe, Notre Dame, Louis Vuitton Foundation, Montmartre, Versailles, took a cruise down the Seine, watched a Lido cabaret, shopped at Champs Elysée and dined at some of the finest restaurants where they served caviar, escargot, duck and *fois gras*. We could buy warm baguettes and coffee from the local cafes or bakeries and walk down the streets without being recognised, except by the odd South Asian tourist who would request Aeram to pose for a selfie. I wanted it to never end.

On our last evening in Paris, we sat on the grass in front of the Notre Dame and watched Japanese tourists get busy with their telephoto lenses to take pictures. It was cold so Aeram wrapped me in his arms. He said, "Please don't ever let me go, Saysha. I cannot live without you." I caressed his cheek with my gloved hand and assured him, "I won't. I love you too much, Aeram." He smiled and kissed me.

Chapter 11

We loved being with just each other, a luxury we hadn't had since we got married because James was always in the background in our home, minds and hearts. I realized that no one could replace Aeram in my life, not even James. I loved James very much but Aeram was my reason to exist. My life had no purpose without him and I could never hurt him again. I felt very protective about him and resolved to distance myself from James if I had to, to ensure Aeram never cried again because of me. By the time, we were on our flight back, I had all but confined James to the recesses of my memory. It was Aeram who brought him back. After a heated mid-air makeout session, while buttoning up his shirt I asked him if James would meet us in Mumbai.

Tears started to form in his eyes. I knew whatever was to come couldn't be good. I held his hand and kissed it. He kissed my forehead. "Saysha, James had an accident when we were in Delhi." The news came as a shock to me. Aeram hurriedly added, "He's okay now. He was in the hospital these few weeks. A car crashed into his BMW. The man in the other car died. James had fractures in his leg, arm and rib and a cut on his head. It happened just after I left Goa to be with you in Delhi."

A headline flashed in my head, "Daniel Albuquerque dies in a car crash." It could have been James Albuquerque. I shuddered at the thought.

Aeram stroked my back and said softly, "Saysha, he is ok. I asked him to join us in Mumbai so he can recuperate. He's able to walk with a crutch right now."

I looked at him and asked, "Was it the same accident which killed Daniel Albuquerque?"

He swallowed hard. "Yes." A tear rolled down his cheek. "Danny tried to kill James."

My mouth opened in horror. "What!" It was loud enough to grab the air-hostess' attention. She came towards us. "Is everything ok, ma'am?"

Meekly, I nodded and held out my glass. She poured water into it: Evian. Aeram waited for her to leave before he started the story:

"Danny was Papa's first cousin. Richard's father was Francis Albuquerque, a mild-mannered man with an English boarding school education and habits. Naturally, he was more into books and music than into looking after estates and accounts. His older brother, George, did all that. Danny was George's only son. George was killed during a drinking brawl when Danny was just eight. Richard was six. Francis treated both as his own and lavished more attention on Danny because he was an orphan. He had lost his mother, Gloria, to malaria when he was only two. Danny, as John Uncle told you, grew up to be a big bully. Georgina Williams was their nanny and Marea would be in and out of the house playing with the boys. She and Richard were very attached to each other even as kids but Danny felt left out so he would tease her or make her do filthy tasks to punish her. When Marea was fourteen, Danny got drunk and tried to force himself on her. Georgina saved her daughter and complained to Francis and Richard's mother, Catherine. They swiftly moved Danny out of there to a boarding school in Mapusa. Marea and Richard loved each other very much. After finishing school, Danny came back to live with them. He was going to Bombay for his college. Marea was a very beautiful young woman. Danny couldn't resist and tried to force himself on her again. This time, Richard saved her and he hit Danny. Richard had never hit anyone before that. He was very mild. Danny, with his bleeding nose, went straight to Father Patrick's house and told him Richard was going to marry Marea. Richard was Catholic and Marea, Protestant. The rest of the story James has told you before. Father Patrick saw to it that they would never marry each other."

"But why did he want to kill James? For the property? He could contest in court. Why kill?" I buried my face in my hands and cried. Aeram put his arm around me. "That is something I haven't figured out, Saysha. I knew he hated James but there had to be something more than property that would be the basis for such hatred. James and I had met Danny just hours before the accident. I had told Danny that I would be going to Delhi for a few days and then we could look at a legal settlement. He was very cordial with me, though he never talked to James, or even looked at him, during the two hours we spent in his lawyer's office in Panjim. James dropped me at the airport and was headed to Albuquerque when the cars collided. It could not be a matter of chance because we had made stops before going to the airport to stock up on petrol and I needed a new charger for my phone. On the return, James had stopped by a friend's house to have a chat before leaving for Old Goa. I am certain Danny had been following every move of James for those three hours. He wanted to kill James. Luckily, James survived with injuries."

I bit my lip. "He was all alone there while we were honeymooning." I felt very guilty.

Aeram kissed me on my shoulder. "It was his idea. I wanted to rush from Delhi to be by his side but he didn't want you to get a whiff of it, of what he had been through."

My whole body was shaking. "Baby, don't cry like this, please."
Aeram held me tight. His lips quivered as he tried to reassure
me that James was okay.

PART 4

MUMBAI

Chapter 12

We walked out of the airport into a jamboree of flashbulbs and fans. Everyone asked us to pose. Random people shook our hands. A porter carried all our bags out in a trolley. And then I finally saw him. James! His one leg was in a cast, his right arm plastered, the top three buttons of his shirt were open, revealing a sling and his forehead was bandaged. He wore a brace around his middle to support the broken rib. James made brokenness look sexy. He smiled at me and I felt all fuzzy and warm inside. Before I could run to him and hug him tight, Aeram beat me to it. The cameras kept clicking as he clung to his brother in tears. James could barely stand, let alone take the weight of another six-footer on him. But Aeram did not let go. He shouted, "I am not going to leave you and go anywhere ever again. Do you fucking understand me?" James stroked his head and patted him on his cheek. This would be media fodder for the next day: The superstar's love for his gay stuntman. He didn't care. I moved close to them and, in full view of the public, hugged them both and then, when finally, Aeram let go of him and composed himself, I hugged James. He held me close and planted kisses on my cheeks.

We moved through a swarm of journalists and fans and headed to the chauffeured limousine that was waiting for us. An Innova would have sufficed but James thought otherwise. I sat between the two men who loved me more than anything else in the world, the two men I loved so dearly and yet so differently. I held James's free hand tight and rested my head on Aeram's shoulder.

Chapter 13

Aeram had to dub for a public announcement video in Andheri so it was just James and me in the apartment. He had moved into the guest bedroom where Aeram usually had his costume trials. James sat on the sofa in my bedroom while I unpacked my suitcase. I had randomly thrown things on the floor and was looking for the lace I had bought from the shops near Montmartre when I heard his chuckle. I turned to see what he was looking at. It was my lingerie, or more specifically a black lace bodice that showed more than it covered. I turned red and gingerly picked it up. My hand stashed it in the recesses of my cupboard. James started laughing. I turned redder. He figured I was embarrassed and left the room.

Half-way through the unpacking, I was tired. I walked over to the patio and plonked myself on the sofa. James brought me coffee. As usual, it was strong, full-bodied, aromatic. He sat next to me. I rested my head on his shoulder. "Where did you learn to make coffee like this?"

He smiled. "I once had a boyfriend who was Turkish. He had come to India to study. He taught me how to make coffee every day, till I got it absolutely right."

"It's really very good, James."

"So are you, Saysha. It's so good to be with you again. I have missed you a lot." He stroked my head and kissed my forehead.

"Have you ever been in a long relationship?" I wanted to know everything about him. He shook his head, "No, the longest was a year I think." Then he wanted to say something but hesitated. I raised my head and looked at him and pressed his hand, "James, tell me, please. I want to know."

"I have always been wary of falling in love, settling down, of permanence, that when the relationship seeks a longer commitment, I just back off. I guess I was scared to fall in love and lose myself to another person… until…until you came along. I never thought I was capable of loving someone so much that it didn't matter that he or she wasn't mine. I love you, Saysha, and I'll love you till the last breath leaves my body."

The 'last breath' might have been three weeks ago. I bit my lip and asked him the question I had been wanting to ask. "Why did Danny want to kill you, James?"

He let out a long sigh. I held his hand. Then he told me:

"After Papa died, Danny came back into the villa and our lives. He claimed that Farah could not inherit the villa because she was a woman and Muslim so he was the only true Christian heir to the Albuquerque clan. He threw all my and Mamma's old stuff out of the spare room and moved in there. He did not contribute to the household finances. Farah had to make ends meet. She had two jobs and three children to feed. One day, Sanam and I were alone at home. Farah had taken Aeram to the doctor because he was sick. Sanam and I were playing in the orchard. We usually steered clear of Danny but that day we were throwing water on each other and in our excitement, we accidentally threw some on Danny. He flew into a rage and was about to hit Sanam but I came in between them. Though he was told that I was Marea's adopted son, I looked too much like Richard and her that he knew I was their bastard child. He dragged me into his room and sodomized me."

I flinched. James pressed my hand.

"That became a pattern, first a few times a month, then a few times a fortnight, then every day. Whenever he flew into a rage and threatened Sanam or Aeram, I offered myself to him. His fury would be spent and he would leave. He started having so much fun that he would sometimes get Father Patrick too. They loved teasing me, the two of them. They would ask me to bend over or do small tasks and then they'd slip their hands into my shorts." James removed his hand from mine, balled his fist, put the thumb in his mouth and bit it hard. He was trying hard to control his tears. I stroked his cheek. He relaxed a little and removed the thumb from his mouth.

"Then one day, Farah found out. She was brave and headstrong. She literally threw Danny out of the house in spite of the fact that he was bigger and got the police to arrest him. She asked her parents to come to Goa to look after us. However, Father Patrick was very influential and got Danny out of jail. Then, during a Sunday Mass, he gave a sermon where he told the churchgoers that the Albuquerque estate was taken over by Muslims. By evening, there was a crowd outside gunning for Farah. She had to leave quickly. Her parents took Aeram and Sanam and her and they left for Panjim. I was in the orchard picking mangoes when they were all gone. They must have searched for me. When I returned home, Danny and Father Patrick were waiting for me. They abused me and kept me as their slave for months. When Farah reached Delhi safely, she filed a petition in court asking for Danny's eviction. The court ruled in her favour and decided that the fate of the property would be decided when the legal heir turned twenty-one. Everyone, except Danny, assumed it was Aeram. When the police came to seal the property, they found me in the guest room unconscious, starving, in rags and covered in blood. I was moved to a missionary school in Mapusa and Farah was intimated about my whereabouts."

James sniffed as he recollected the rest of the story. It was as fresh in his memory as if it had happened the day before.

"Father Patrick had many friends in that school. They abused me over and over again. They thought I would kill myself out of shame. But after a point I did not care anymore. I even started enjoying it. They tried to break me but couldn't. I had triumphed. Then one day, I fell in love with a boy from our soccer team. When the coach found out, he sounded the alarm and I was kicked out by the very same people who had abused me those three years. I came back to Mamma's house in the orchard. Thankfully, Danny had moved to Mumbai and Father Patrick had gone to Ponda. I had to find all kinds of work to just survive. Gradually, I found love among other men like me. Farah must have kept looking for me, trying to get me to join them in Delhi but after a point, it must have become difficult for her to keep track of me. I kept a low profile and moved between Goa, Mumbai, Pune and Bangalore.

"When I turned twenty-one, Danny came back to the villa but it was still sealed. He then realized that Aeram and not I was the heir. He rented a property down the road and waited there till Aeram's twenty-first birthday. He would keep coming from Mumbai once or twice a month to check on the villa. I steered clear of him. Then when Aeram started renovating the property, it grabbed headlines. Danny realized he couldn't fight

Aeram in court so he laid low until he stumbled upon the old clause put down by Xavier during the Inquisition. He figured Aeram could not be Richard's heir and assumed I was dead or missing so he put in his claim to it. He did not know I was alive till a couple of months ago when Aeram submitted Papa's second will in court. Danny hated me on four counts: One, I am Richard and Marea's son. Two, I own the property. Three, that in spite of all his efforts to degrade me to less than an animal and kill my self-esteem, I am still alive and proud of who I am. Four, that only I knew what a beast of a man he was and that could ruin his chances of getting a ticket for the elections. He couldn't dream of killing Aeram because he's too rich and powerful and famous. But me, he tried and failed, again."

Tears streamed down James's cheeks. I cradled his head in my palms and he broke down. At that moment, Aeram walked in. He watched us. Then he poured a glass of water and brought it to James. He drank the water and kissed Aeram on his forehead, like a father would kiss a son. Aeram knelt on the floor on both his knees and put his head on James's knee just above his cast. James stroked his head. A tear rolled down Aeram's cheek. He whispered, "I love you." James stroked Aeram's cheek and said, "I love you too." Then he wiped off his brother's tears with his thumb. Here were two macho men, known for their brute strength and vanity expressing their love to each other.

I broke the silence with a question. "So now that Danny's no more, there will be no contesting the property, right?"

Aeram raised his head to look at me and answered, "There's one more person who is interested in our estate. The one who wants it more than Danny ever did. Danny was just his pawn. We'll have to deal with the kingpin now. Father Patrick is back in Old Goa as Archbishop at Sé Catedral de Santa Catarina. And he's going to hit us where it hurts most."

A shiver ran down my spine. Aeram let out a sigh and rested his head on James's knee again. James threw his head back and laughed. "Oh, I so want to punch him in the face. Finally!" He clapped his free hand onto the sofa's arm-rest.

We all laughed.

Chapter 14

I lay in bed unable to sleep. It was well past midnight. What James had told me was a gut-wrenching story of abuse and rape. I had never met anyone who had been subject to such inhuman treatment before. It had always felt so distant from the sheltered world Mom and Dad had provided for my brother and me.

I curled into a ball and cried. Aeram woke up.

He stroked my head and asked, "Saysha, what's the matter?"

I sobbed.

"Please," he begged me and pressed his body close to mine.

"I can't even imagine what he must have gone through or felt through all those years." I cried loud.

Aeram stiffened a little. He whispered, "I can."

I looked at him. His lips were trembling and he clenched and opened his fists a few times. He did that when he was anxious or angry about something.

What came out of his mouth was barely audible. "I can, because I have gone through it."

If I could scream, I would have.

He looked at me and asked, "Remember when I told you I have a connection with James that I can't have with anyone else, not even you?"

I nodded.

"Well," he softly said, "we both know the same pain."

He fell back down on the pillow, placed one hand over his head, shut his eyes as if he were replaying everything in his head and started talking:

"I was always the pretty boy in school; fair, with thin and slender limbs like a girl's, hairless body and cheeks that turned pink when the temperature rose just slightly. We had moved to New Delhi just after my sixth birthday. It was a new place and a new school. People spoke differently and teased me because of my looks. I spoke only English and could understand a little Konkani. My classmates in school spoke mostly Hindi, Punjabi and little English. They mocked me whenever I attempted to speak Hindi."

He sniffed. I stroked his arm. His eyes remained shut while he continued:

"Naturally, I missed Goa and James. He was our protector. He always fought the bullies and he had never lost a fight. Nobody messed with James even then. Ammi told Sanam and me that he would join us later. We kept waiting for him, me, more than anyone else. Ammi intended to go back to Albuquerque in secret and look for him. Then the police in Goa informed her that James had been moved to a boarding school in Mapusa. She was relieved that she at least knew where he was and made an old friend of hers, his local guardian. They kept in touch with each other. When I was seven, Ammi agreed to marry her cousin Ibrahim, who became my stepfather. He had accepted her with two kids but made it clear he didn't want a third one so James was forced to stay in the boarding school in Mapusa. Ammi wanted to move him to Delhi after he turned fifteen. Feroz, my stepfather's son from his previous wife, would visit us from time to time. I was seven, he was seventeen. He once fondled me and since I did not know what it was, I felt ashamed and kept it to myself. His visits increased and I became more and more withdrawn. I stopped talking altogether, hardly ate and cried in my sleep. It went on for months. Initially, Ammi thought it was because she had remarried and I had a difficult time accepting Ibrahim as my father. But it wasn't that. Richard had been a distant father to me because I reminded him of Marea's death. My only guardian since infancy was James because Ammi was very busy working two jobs and managing my sick father."

Aeram was talking to me but I sensed he wanted James to be near him. He continued, with his eyes closed, "One afternoon, Ammi caught Feroz touching me. His hand was inside my shorts. She immediately knew what was wrong and threatened my stepfather with divorce if Feroz ever entered the house again. He was sent to a college in America. The day he boarded the flight to Chicago, I was so relieved that after months, I slept through the night. There were no nightmares about him trying to get into my bed under my sheet next to me."

He was crying. "Hey, please don't cry, Aeram," I whispered, wiping away his tears. He broke down and wailed. I held him tight but he didn't stop. I got out of bed and poured him a glass of water. He didn't take it. Instead, he brought his knees to his chin and desperately tried to muffle his screams.

There was a knock on the door. I half-opened it to find James. He was wearing only his black soccer shorts. James ran his eyes over me. I was wearing a white lace negligee that barely covered anything. He averted his gaze and glanced at Aeram who was sobbing inconsolably. "I heard his cries. Do you need me here?" James asked me while I hurriedly grabbed Aeram's blue shirt that he had thrown on the floor and draped it around my shoulders. "Yes, James. He was telling me about Feroz," I whispered, not sure whether James knew the whole story. He didn't ask, just hobbled in and sat on the bed next to Aeram, stretching his legs. Aeram clung to him and cried his heart out. James didn't say a word. He stroked Aeram's head with his free hand. I stood at the foot of the bed looking at the two of them wondering what I should do next.

"Sit there, Saysha," James instructed me, pointing towards the other side of the bed, next to Aeram. I did. Aeram, who was resting his head on James's bare chest above the rib-brace, turned to see me with teary half-open eyes. His lips were quivering. After several quiet minutes, he composed himself and started telling me the rest of the story. I tried to stop him because it would only cause him more distress but he wanted to let it all out. He sat up between James and me. James put his free left arm protectively around his brother's shoulder. He sniffed before speaking:

"When I was about ten, the maths teacher, Mr Sylva, took an interest in me. He would slip his hand inside my shirt on the pretext of patting my back. If he caught me talking or doing something which he thought was wrong, he would call me into the staff room after school hours and cane me on my buttocks till they were red. He always wanted to look at how well he had done the job."

James's jaw tightened. He put his bandaged head on Aeram's and gently kissed his brother's hair. Then he closed his eyes while Aeram narrated the rest of the story:

"After many beatings. I found the courage to complain to Ammi. She threatened the school with a lawsuit and so Mr Sylva was expelled. It made news as well. But the damage had been done. I was wary of people, hardly talked and never made friends. Ammi asked me to focus on my studies and sports. She became extremely protective of me and took a keen interest in the PTA. Over a period of time, I started liking dramatics because I could play parts and characters I wasn't. It gave me a new identity. I liked my sports teacher Colonel Singh, a retired army officer, and opted for all kinds of sports; athletics, hockey, football and cricket. I became bigger, bulkier and stronger and people realised they could no longer mess with me. I would fight off all the bullies."

James opened his eyes, tousled Aeram's hair and laughed. Aeram managed a weak smile. He looked down and said, "The girls stayed away from me because of my reputation of being arrogant and hot-headed. I just couldn't trust anyone to make friends. I still can't." He shook his head and shrugged. James stroked his hair and whispered, "It's okay, Aeram. I'm there. I'll always be with you." Aeram smiled meekly.

Then he turned towards me. "Over three years of college, Saysha, you were the first person to sit with me in the canteen and have lunch. You wiped the sauce from my lips. When your fingers touched them, I wanted to kiss them."

He smiled at the memory. Caressing my cheek, he said, "God! I have loved you since that moment, Saysha. You became my centre of gravity. That is why I am so possessive and protective about you. I can't see you with anyone else, anywhere else but in my arms." He glanced at James who had shut his eyes again.

I gave him a peck on his cheek. "But," he continued, "what I have gone through is nothing compared to what he has gone through." He pointed at James, who kissed him on the forehead and whispered, "I love you, darling." Then James's eyes bored into my soul and he declared, "I love you more than anything in the world."

Chapter 15

Finally, it was the day of our wedding anniversary. Since our wedding had been such a secret affair, we wanted to have a big anniversary party. Zarine, from Aeram's PR team, took charge of everything — venue, food, guest lists, invites, press, entertainment, games — all of it. Aeram and I just nodded to whatever she said. Secretly, we wanted just the two of us somewhere. But this was needed. Over the last year, we had many complaints from friends and family that we had married in secret and not thrown a party.

It was also the first time my parents flew over to Mumbai to stay with us. Dad was impressed. Mom was pleased that I had made it my own. Sanam moved to the bedroom downstairs while James turned the gym into a bedroom with a bean bag and Mom and Dad moved into the guest bedroom upstairs. Vikram couldn't join us because he had exams in Delhi.

As our anniversary date approached, I started getting the jitters. Mom took over to coordinate with Zarine, James handled the logistics and Sanam decided to become my stylist.

That evening, I dressed in a red Shantanu and Nikhil off-shoulder gown and stood next to Aeram who wore a black tuxedo. He looked so divine that I only hoped I looked decent enough next to him. "Gosh! You're so beautiful, Saysha," he gushed and kissed my cheek. We were posing for some family photos Dad insisted on clicking, when James walked in. He looked sleek in a dark grey suit and shirt of the same colour with the top two buttons undone. His leg cast had come off but he had to wear a brace around his middle and his arm was still in a plaster. He walked up to me, took my hand in his and kissed it. "You look ravishing, Saysha." Then he turned to Aeram and gave him a key. "Your anniversary gift is in Alhandra in Portugal. Make sure to stop over there before you head to the US."

Aeram and I were so surprised we shouted in chorus, "What?"

James winked, "It's my house, baby. I can give it to whoever I want."

My parents and Sanam had no clue what he was talking about. They just smiled.

The venue of our anniversary gala was the Brabourne Stadium at the Cricket Club of India. Since we had decided on a big celebration, Aeram had left no stone unturned to make it the party of the year. The who's who of Mumbai, Delhi, Goa and even some of his Hollywood friends were invited. The stadium's stands were decorated with lights. Shweta

Raisinghani, one of India's best art directors and my boss, had done the whole place up, keeping in mind the Venetian theme. It brought back memories of the Venetian masquerade ball in my college in Shimla where Aeram had dressed as Batman and had unexpectedly revealed himself. The cascade of events had culminated in our secret court marriage. This time, we had left the masquerade out. There were too many well-known faces who wanted to show the world they were there for the party of the year.

The biggest attraction was a gondola ride in an artificial canal, made out of floats that were filled with water, along the perimeter of the ground. There were lighted arches over it. As Aeram and I floated in the gondola, a cheer went up. He kissed me under one of the lighted arches sending the paparazzi in a tizzy. The gondola then docked right next to the platform that was to be the stage for the evening. No one had ever made an entrance on a boat in the middle of a cricket stadium!

While Dad regaled the audience with anecdotes of how Aeram and he had met the first time when he had come to our house on Valentine's Day, my eyes searched for James. Finally, I found him in the far corner of the field near the buffet chatting with a thin man with salt-and-pepper hair. He looked very plain in the middle of the swish-set we had invited which included the film fraternity, industrialists, media, politicians, army generals and top bureaucrats. Even from the distance I could make out that their conversation was serious. I was looking at them, when Rachel stood in my way. "Saysha, you look fabulous!" I blushed. She had put on a bit of weight since we had last met in Goa, the side-effect of being a pastry chef at one of the country's top hotels. She had worn black to camouflage her curves.

I enquired, "Where's Lionel?"

"At sea. Will come after two weeks," she replied. Then she turned around and stood next to me. "Girl, it's your anniversary bash and you're looking at him?" Her finger pointed towards James.

I coloured and looked away. She pretended not to notice. "I know man, even with all those broken appendages, that man is sexy." A pair of lips touched my right cheek. It was Aeram.

"Who is sexy?" He asked.

Rachel swallowed hard. I giggled and told Aeram, "Rachel says, even with all those broken appendages, James looks sexy."

She rolled her eyes.

Aeram mocked us, "You two are ogling at my sexy gay stunt-double. It's my anniversary bash! Come on!"

Rachel said in her singsong voice, "Well, the girls want to have some fun, Aeram. And not a bloody gondola ride."

Aeram responded in his after-sex voice, "Well, there's a buffet, Rachel. Go sink your teeth into some flesh."

I punched him.

"Ow, Saysha," he yelped.

"This one's a prude, Aeram. I am not, so I am going all out today. See you." She blew a kiss at us and left.

Aeram felt a tap on his shoulder. It was his director, Shan. He was wearing a blue sofa upholstery-like designer suit with big sunflower print with matching large blue glasses and red shoes. I didn't like him but had to tolerate him because Aeram had signed not one but three films with the man. He kissed me and hugged me. James caught my eye. My knight in shining armour was coming to rescue me from a conversation I didn't want to have. "Hi Shan," shouted James. Shan grimaced. He hated James ever since the latter had turned down his overtures. He whispered, "Hi." James was a stunt-double, a small fry to care for among the big fish there. James held my hand and led me away with just an, "Excuse us." Aeram laughed. Shan frowned. James hooked my arm in his and walked me over towards the plain-looking man he had been talking to. He did the introductions. "This is Saysha, Aeram's wife, and this is Manohar Salgaonkar, our lawyer. He is a very old friend of Farah and Richard's and is managing the legal stuff for all our estates. Manohar *mama* was also my local guardian when I was in the boarding school in Mapusa after Farah, Aeram and Sanam left for Delhi. Farah paid my fees through him and he would take me home on weekends whenever I was allowed to leave the hostel."

I looked at the man in plain light grey Raymonds suit with renewed respect and touched his feet. He tried to stop me.

"Aeram's choice is excellent," he said, bobbing his head. James smiled in acknowledgement. He then pointed to the buffet and spoke in Konkani. Manohar Uncle headed towards the tables leaving James and me alone for the first time that night. He ran his eyes over me, from head to toe. "Saysha," he said in a very sexy deep voice and took me in his arms. He held me very tight, very close with his plastered arm and gently ran his tongue across the length of my collar bone and kissed me on my neck. "I love you so much." Then he loosened his hold of me and walked away. I wished he would hold me like that forever.

The DJ announced the dances after people were sufficiently drunk to move on their own. I danced with Aeram. He kissed me on my lips during each dance. James danced with Tia,

Sanam and Joe. When the slow dance section came, Imran came over to ask Aeram for his leave. Aeram kissed my hand and told me he would see Imran off and be right back in minutes. I watched James dance with Sanam. When the second song started, he passed her on to Dad and walked towards me. I remembered the last time someone had replaced Aeram on the dance floor and tried to dance with me, he had grabbed the guy with his collar and literally shaken him up. James stretched out his free hand. I hesitated to take it. "Come on," he mouthed the words. Cautiously, I put my hand in his and he pulled me close, very close. I watched Rachel from the corner of my eye. She was making out with Cyrus, one of the tech wizards on Aeram's team. James put his lips near my ear. "It's ok," he whispered. I relaxed a little and put my head on his chest. He held me tight. Since he couldn't move much, we just stayed in that position through Marc Anthony's song, *You Sang to Me*. Then suddenly, he loosened his hold and walked away, leaving me alone on the floor. After two minutes, Aeram came next to me. "I am sorry baby, I kept you away from the floor so long," he said in his sexy voice and twirled me on the floor. A cheer rose. James whistled and clapped for us.

We danced till the wee hours of the morning. Someone decided to use the makeshift canal as a swimming pool. Soon people were jumping in and wetting their designer gear that would have cost most people both their kidneys. By the time we stumbled into our home, all of us were drunk, except James. He never had a sip of alcohol when he knew Aeram and I would go crazy with our drinking.

Chapter 16

The week was spent showing my parents the sights of Mumbai, taking them to one of Aeram's shoots where Dad was really impressed with his vanity van, taking Sanam and Mom to shop at expensive boutiques and restaurants and taking Dad to meet his colleagues in the army. James, since he was still recuperating from his injuries, accompanied us only sometimes.

Then, it was their last day in town. Aeram had gone with Sanam to her therapist. Mom and Dad were napping in the bedroom. They had just finished packing. Their flight was in the evening. Rachel had delivered boxes of chocolates and brownies she had made as send-off gifts for them. I was tidying up the dining table after an hour of sketching when James walked in. His plaster had been cut and now both his hands were free. He still limped a little and had to wear the brace for his rib but he looked almost normal. He smiled and came towards me. Then he saw the box of chocolates. I offered him one. He picked it up but offered it to me. I was going to take it from his hand, when he asked me to open my mouth. I did and he placed the chocolate in. But he didn't remove his thumb. He rolled the chocolate in my mouth with his thumb all over my inner cheek, gums and tongue. A knot started to form in my stomach. Then slowly he moved his thumb out of my mouth and ran it over my lips. It gave me goosebumps. He smiled and walked off sucking his thumb while I held the box of chocolates. The man knew how to make love with minimal contact. And that made me insane.

That evening, the house was empty again. Aeram had left for Delhi to take Sanam home and meet with a tech company CEO. James went to drop them at the airport. To take my mind off everything, I decided to hit the gym. Forty-five minutes into my training schedule, I was sweating buckets, when James walked in. I had forgotten that he had camped there when my parents were around. He took a good look at me. I was panting from all that running. So much for partying through the week! He went to the refrigerator and got some ice and stood opposite me while I was doing my stretches. He seductively sucked at the ice watching me. I turned red. Then he ran the same cube on my sweaty upper lip and sucked it.

"Eww, James, you're so gross!" I squirmed.

He did it again.

I stepped away.

He started laughing.

"Not funny, James."

He pulled me towards him and put his forehead to mine. His lips were just an inch away from my mouth. He blew on my lips gently. It sent a shiver down my body. Then, in his deep sexy voice, he said, "You have no idea how much I want to kiss you right now but I have promised him that I won't ever. I cannot not do anything about it, even if it's gross." He put the ice cube in his mouth and walked away.

I lay tossing and turning in bed that night as the events of the day replayed in my head. It was 1 am. I texted Aeram:

Saysha: I miss you so much. Please come to me. Please.

I sent it and after it got delivered, I realized that I had mistakenly sent it to James. Damn!

I lay quietly in bed hoping James was fast asleep in the guest room next door. He had moved upstairs from the gym.

There was a knock on my door.

I wrapped a gown over my black silk pyjama shorts and tank top and opened the door.

James was in shorts and a vest.

"What's the matter, Saysha?" He asked.

I looked down. "It's embarrassing James. I actually wrote that to Aeram but sent it to you by mistake."

He smiled. "Ok, good night," he said and turned to leave. He lingered at the door for a minute and said, "Call me if you need anything."

I nodded. I lay in bed for another hour tossing and turning. Then I got out of the room, and made my way to the lounge in the patio. James was there, lying on the couch. He got up when he saw me.

"Still can't sleep?"

I shook my head.

He asked me, "Have you had sleep issues before?"

I nodded. "When I broke up with Aeram and moved to the college in Shimla, I hardly slept through the three years. The first time I met him again, I slept peacefully."

"Oh dear!" He sighed.

Then he asked, "Want a massage?"

I raised my brow.

"Just a massage, Saysha. I am not asking to have sex with you." He smirked.

I laughed.

I took off my robe and he came out of the kitchen with some olive oil.

As his fingers worked my hair, I started to relax, almost drowse off. The man was so talented. "Where did you learn this?"

"Well, in Goa, one of the better ways to make quick money is to give tourists massages on the beach. You get five or six clients and you can make anywhere between Rs 10-15000 a day. Even if you have to share it with the hotels, it still is a good deal."

"Wow! You and Aeram have so many talents and interests. I hardly have one of two. I still don't know why Aeram picked me over any other girl."

James sat on the coffee table opposite me and held both my hands. "The fact that you exist is good enough for the two of us. Talents are distractions. You acquire them to hide your innate flaws, to show the world that you're more than the soul and body you own. But Saysha, you're perfect just the way you're made. You don't need talent. You've got such a beautiful soul."

I blushed at the compliment.

He raised my leg and put it on his lap. Then he sucked my big toe on the right foot. A current ran through my body jolting me upright.

"James please don't, I pleaded."

He blew on it gently.

"James please," I begged him.

"Ok." He smiled and poured some oil on the palm of his hand. Then he started massaging my foot and leg. I started to relax again.

"How do you even call yourself gay if you're into all this?"

He chuckled. "What makes you think men don't like doing this?"

I turned red.

He continued, "Besides, I still prefer men to women. It's only you, Saysha. I want to try things with you." He seductively licked his lower lip. "And if you didn't enjoy them half as much as you do, I wouldn't have dared." He winked at me.

I was too embarrassed to even look at him.

He was enjoying himself. "You know, you could learn a few things from me and try them on him."

I kicked him right on his broken rib

"Ouch! You're a toughie."

That didn't stop him from talking, though. "I have a lot more experience with sex than the two of you put together."

I didn't doubt that. Aeram and I had never kissed anyone before each other. And I had kissed only one man other than him, the one who was massaging my foot.

Curiosity got the better of me and I asked him, "How many people have you slept with?"

He chuckled. "I stopped counting after a hundred."

I was shocked. "What? You've slept with over hundred people!"

He threw his head back and laughed. Then he became serious the very next minute and said, "I had to sell sex to survive after I got kicked out of school."

I shuddered at the thought.

He chuckled. "Don't worry. I get myself tested every year for VD, HIV, Hepatitis."

It hadn't even crossed my mind that he could have had one of those diseases.

His fingers were working on my calves. He whispered, "You're so beautiful, Saysha."

I relaxed and closed my eyes. Then he laughed.

I opened my eyes. "What?"

"We have quite a situation, you know."

I raised my eyebrows.

He elaborated, "Aeram loves me much more than he loves you though he will never admit it. I love you much more than I love him and I have admitted it. And you, you almost love us both the same yet differently." A smile played on his lips. "If you ever have to choose, Saysha, will it be him or me?"

I sat upright and removed my leg from his lap. Angrily, I asked, "Why do you want me to choose?"

He smirked. "It's just a question."

I didn't answer.

His gaze pierced my heart.

Then very coldly he said, "If it ever comes to a choice, choose only him. I have wounds that haven't healed and I can't show those to anyone, not even you."

"Can we stop talking about this?" I admonished him.

He got up and sat right next to me. I noticed he wasn't wearing his brace. My kick might have hurt his rib a lot more than he showed.

James put his arm around me and kissed my forehead. "I won't ever leave you, Saysha, so you'll never have to choose between us."

I turned to him and asked a question that had been playing in my head for days: "If Danny hadn't sodomized you, you might have been straight, right?"

He sighed. "I don't know. I might have been straight or I might not. Many gay people I have met have had some kind of childhood experience of abuse. But that's not to say they all become gay. I have met people who have been brought up with a lot of love and care and are gay as well. It's an individual's make or choice or both, I guess. People call me abnormal because I am gay but I am more sorted in my head and about my identity than that husband of yours who is straight. He is a superstar, but doesn't enjoy being one. He loves you like crazy but is so possessive about you that he suffocates you. He is brilliant in many ways but absolutely foolish when it comes to relationships. He doesn't trust anybody so he cannot make friends. He loves making money but doesn't know how to spend it on things that give him satisfaction. He has the world at his feet and still isn't happy. Aeram has a few loose screws up there," he laughed. I giggled. That was true, Aeram had said so himself. He could never be normal. James, on the other hand, owned his identity and sexuality with pride. He was as normal as normal would allow.

The next morning, when Aeram walked in, he found James and me on two separate sofas on the patio. He picked me up and took me to the bedroom. When I woke up, I found him lying naked next to me, spooning me.

I replayed the conversation with James in my head. Aeram and I had lots of sex but we never talked about it. James and I always talked about sex but we had never done it.

Chapter 17

If there was one party I really didn't want to attend, it was Shan's. The man just got on my nerves. He leered at Aeram, had felt James up and wanted to hug and kiss me whenever we met. James would have sat it out if Aeram hadn't been adamant about me attending it. Since Shan was one of industry's biggest snobs, he wanted all his guests to dress in their finest. Sanam, my on-call stylist, suggested Armani or Valentino. I wore Masaba instead. Shan would definitely be in florals. Masaba's bold handprints would be the best for this party, I thought. Both Aeram and James dressed identically. They were clad in black top-to-toe; black shirts, black fitted trousers, black shoes and black blazers. They looked like they were part of a Bond movie. The top three buttons of James's shirt were open and revealed his gold Cross.

During our drive to Bandra, I watched the moonlight fall over James's features. He saw me admiring him and smiled. I looked away.

Shan greeted all of us with hugs and air-kisses, even James. Then he took Aeram by hand and led him to the other side of the room to meet a couple of foreigners, leaving James and me unattended. There were many members of the press. Shan's party theme was Hollywood so the men were dressed appropriately. I felt a bit out of place. I should have gone with Sanam's suggestions. James asked me if I wanted a drink. "Wine, white, please," I whispered. He nodded and left. I took a seat next to an older actress, Sona, who glanced at me and then went back to chatting with her friends. I felt so out of place that I wanted to leave. Then Aeram came towards me with Imran and Sanghamitra. We hugged each other and Sangha took me around the room to introduce me to other actors and actresses. When Shweta walked in, I finally found someone other than James I could talk to. We were chatting about something when behind me a couple of pretty young things started making fun of my outfit. I felt very embarrassed. Shweta didn't notice. She was talking about the schedules for the new period film. Then someone called her from the other side of the room and she left me. The girls behind me were loud. "She's a superstar's wife and she's interning with an art director. How sad is that! If I had married Aeram, I would have asked Imran to direct a movie with me in it." The girl laughed. I turned around and glared at her. It was Aeram's co-star, Aditi, who Shan was launching in their new film. They were rumoured to be very close. Aditi's father, one of the city's leading diamond merchants, had financed Shan's first film. She put on her fake smile and pushed me away to make her way towards Shan, Aeram and Imran. I shuddered when she planted a kiss on Aeram's cheek. She used her index finger to rub off the pink lipstick stain.

I was going to give her a piece of my mind when James stood in my way and said, "Let's take a walk outside. It's kind of stuffy in here." When I didn't move, he held my hand and pulled me away, "Come on." Aditi watched us leave and giggled. James turned around. Their eyes met. She stopped laughing and left Aeram's side. Nobody messed with James.

James walked me out of the bungalow's big gates to the main road, right towards the promenade. He unstrapped my heels and carried them as we made our way among the tetrapods that broke the waves. We sat there in silence. The waves made their music. He texted Aeram, "Saysha and I are sitting on the tetrapods across the road. Come join us when you've had too much of that idiot."

James ran his hand through his hair. His Cross glistened in the moonlight. I reached for it. "It's beautiful," I whispered, running my thumb over it.

He scoffed and told me, "It's really old."

"Interesting. How old?"

"It belonged to Afonso de Albuquerque. When he set out on his journey towards India to conquer the spice trade from the Arabs, King Manuel I of Portugal bestowed it on him. This Cross is shaped like the flag of the Casa da Índia, the Portuguese commercial organization Manuel I created during the Age of Discovery. It administered the Portuguese Empire's territories in India, Africa, and Asia. There were three identical crosses: One for Vasco da Gama, who discovered the sea route to India, another for Pedro Álvares Cabral, who discovered Brazil, and this was Afonso de Albuquerque's who established the Portuguese hegemony in the Indian Ocean. This family heirloom has passed from one generation to another to the heir to the estate and title."

He had regurgitated a chapter out of a history textbook. Never before had I heard a driver use the word 'hegemony'. I looked at the Cross in my palm and asked, "Did Richard give it to you?"

James nodded and said, "Before he died. He marked me as its guardian and also the guardian of all the estates and my siblings."

I wondered aloud, "And yet, you have to fight to get what you actually own."

James shrugged. "Don't we all fight for something? Love, name, job, property, fame, identity, independence, sexuality, choice, rights, life, we all have to fight for something, right?"

He kissed the Cross. "Danny badly wanted this. I had hidden it in Mamma's old house. It costs a fortune. The other two crosses have disappeared down the centuries, probably locked away in some private collectors' vaults."

I touched the Cross on his chest. He placed his hand on mine. I could feel his heartbeats.

He changed the subject. "Aditi was making fun of you. Had it been a guy, I would have punched him in the face."

I stroked his chest and told him, "I am glad you didn't hit her. She was drunk."

He shook his head. "I don't hit women, Saysha. But I might have given her a piece of my mind. She's very buddy-buddy with Shan."

"You don't like him at all."

"No, absolutely not!" There was a sharpness in his tone. "The man is a bully, Saysha. He thinks that just because he's rich and famous and supposedly popular in the fraternity, he can get away with feeling people up and exploiting them. If Aeram hadn't signed those films with him, I would have beaten the shit out of the bastard that he would not even look at an animal again, let alone a man or a woman."

We were interrupted by a vendor who was selling ice-cream. James asked me if I wanted one. I nodded. He bought two. The taste of plain vanilla brought back memories of a simpler life in Delhi when I was a nobody. I licked the cone the second time when James moved in to lick it too. Our tongues touched. A tingling sensation worked through my stomach. He winked at me and licked his ice-cream.

"You're so gross, James," I shouted at him.

He said in his husky voice, "I like playing dirty." When I finished my ice-cream, he cradled my head with both his hands and ran his tongue along my lips to lick off the remnants of the ice-cream. It gave me goosebumps. "I didn't kiss you. I just didn't want to waste such good ice-cream."

The phone buzzed. It was Aeram. We located the car and went to pick him up. Aeram and I made out in the backseat while James drove us home. He caught my eye a couple of times and then looked away.

Chapter 18

As with most things with Aeram, he broke the news of going to New York over breakfast very casually and very suddenly. "We're leaving tomorrow," he said.

James looked up from his bowl of *poha* and then observed my reaction. He obviously knew everything much before I did.

"For how long?" I asked Aeram.

He shrugged. "About two weeks. Add travel time of a couple of days on either side and a stopover at Lisbon."

James smiled.

Aeram looked at him. "Thanks to you."

James blew him a kiss and winked. Then he looked at me.

I asked him, "You'll be coming with us this time, right?"

He shook his head. "No, I am going to be in Goa."

A chill ran down my spine. The last time we were away in Delhi and Paris and he was in Goa alone, it had nearly killed him. This time, his adversary was the most powerful of them all, the Archbishop of Goa and Daman, Father Patrick.

He sensed my uneasiness and put his hand on mine. "I'll be okay, Saysha, I promise," and after putting a spoonful of *poha* in his mouth, added, "besides, Father Patrick is in his late seventies so I don't think he's going to be driving cars under the influence of alcohol and cocaine."

Aeram laughed. I did not find it funny. His phone was ringing. Sanam was calling him. He rose from the table to answer and told us, "I'll be back." James put my hand to his lips and kissed it. Then he sucked my thumb. I stifled my moans. Then suddenly he let go of my hand and said, "Don't worry about me. I have you." He smacked his lips, picked up the dishes from the table and went into the kitchen. I felt a peck on my cheek. It was Aeram.

"Sanam might join us in New York. James, come, please." Aeram begged him. From the other side of the kitchen's glass partition, I could see James shaking his head. "Okay, then we can go, like, maybe three weeks later," Aeram suggested.

James came out of the kitchen and grabbed his brother's shirt by its collar. The latter winced. He put his face really close to Aeram's, their noses almost touching. James hissed, "You will leave tomorrow. You don't make plans. I do." My husband meekly nodded. I had never seen anyone talk to Aeram like that. He had never shown fear, until then. James let go of his shirt, caressed his cheek and kissed him on the forehead. Aeram relaxed a little. James smiled at me and said, "Get packing, Saysha."

This whole year, I had believed that Aeram was the boss and James the employee until he revealed who the real boss was. I thought I knew everything about the men I loved until that moment.

Chapter 19

Packing for over two weeks with just a day's warning was a huge task for me. Aeram was busy in his study calling his agent in New York and making last-minute arrangements. I looked at the heaps of clothes on my bed and buried my head in them. I needed time to do things. And with Aeram, things moved too quickly.

James walked in. "Saysha, what's the matter?" He sat next to me on a heap of laundered clothes and took my hands in his.

I sniffed, "This is all so sudden."

James chuckled. "Only you, Saysha. Nobody else would cry when they're offered a chance to go on a holiday."

I punched him.

"Ow, Saysha!" Then he got all serious. "Is that the only reason you were crying?"

"I'm worried about you, James." It was killing me.

He cupped my face in his palms and kissed me on my forehead. "Ok, I promise you I will come to New York once I am finished with the work in Goa." I felt his breath on my lips.

"Promise?"

"Yes, promise."

He traced his thumb on my lip and thrust it in my mouth. This time, he reached deep inside and caressed the length of my tongue. "Bite me."

What?

I tried to get his thumb out of my mouth but he thrust it in again. He looked into my eyes, "Bite me so hard that it bleeds like you bite your lip."

I bit him.

"Harder."

I bit him harder. He winced. I tasted blood, his blood. He withdrew his thumb and sucked it.

When it stopped bleeding, he told me, "Remember this, Saysha, the taste of my blood. When you want to punish yourself by biting your lip, remember what this tasted like. Don't be hard on yourself, Saysha. I cannot see you bleed."

He kissed my cheek.

"Why are you not coming with us?" I had to ask him just one more time before we left.

He sighed.

"My fight against Father Patrick and the church is my own. My love for you is my only weakness and nobody but Aeram knows about it. That's why I want you both to leave the country. When you go to Alhandra near Lisbon, I'll get two days to prepare for the shitstorm that will come my way. Father Patrick is mad at me. He has lost Danny. He may be an old man but he's very cunning. He likes theatre. He will strip me of my dignity before everyone but not all at once. He'll do it the way he used to take off my school uniform. He would take a long time to open one button of my shirt after another and keep his fingers on my chest forever."

A tear rolled down his cheek.

"He's waiting for the moment Aeram leaves for the US. It has been out in the papers for a while. He knows that without Aeram's money and power, I'll be defenceless. When Aeram's PR drops news of your arrival in New York, it will be the day he'll strike."

I flinched.

James wasn't done yet. "Father Patrick saw to it that Papa and Mamma led miserable lives. He saw to it that all three of us remained bastards and couldn't be baptized as infants. He drove my second mother, Farah, out of her own home never to return. He is the reason I met my brother after fifteen years in the most miserable state. He has destroyed our family, our dignity, our childhood and our name just because of his greed and I, the true son of Richard Albuquerque will make him pay and pay dearly."

The skeptic in me spoke. "You think you'll be able to do that in two weeks?"

"We don't have a choice. If we don't do it now, we may lose them all," he replied. Then, he whispered, more to himself than to me from Psalm 23:

"Even though I walk

through the darkest valley,

I will fear no evil,

for you are with me;

your rod and your staff,

they comfort me.

You prepare a table before me

in the presence of my enemies.

You anoint my head with oil;

my cup overflows.

Surely your goodness and love will follow me

all the days of my life,

and I will dwell in the house of the Lord

forever."

He kissed me on my cheek and said, "Nobody messes with James, Saysha. Don't read the news till you come back from New York. Enjoy your time in Lisbon. I want you to redesign the property at Alhandra."

With that, he left, leaving me with heaps of clothes and lots to worry about.

PART 5

ALHANDRA

Chapter 20

The spectacular view of the Marina de Alhandra from the living room of the four-bedroom Albuquerque villa in Alhandra in Portugal, is what we walked into having arrived after a long Lufthansa flight to Lisbon from Mumbai. The house was on the corner between Avenue Souza Martins and Avenue Baptista Perreira and had been renovated by Richard's father, Francis Albuquerque in the 1960s.

Like many old Goan Portuguese families, Richard's ancestors had envisioned a situation where they might not live in Goa forever so they had bought prime properties along Portugal's coast. Alhandra, the birthplace of Afonso de Albuquerque, was Richard's great-grandfather, Minguel de Albuquerque's choice. This was to be our home for the next couple of days.

The old caretaker, Ana, had left a box of chocolates in the bedroom. They looked like the ones Rachel had once gifted us. I picked one and put it in Aeram's mouth and did not pull out my thumb. I rolled the chocolate all the way inside and on the sides of his inner cheeks. He moaned with pleasure. Then I rubbed his lips with chocolate and sucked my thumb. He ran his tongue on his lips. He had enjoyed that. "Where did you learn this from?" "I saw it somewhere," I told him nonchalantly. "Do it again," he pressed my hand. James was right. I could learn a few things from him and try them on Aeram. He certainly knew more about how to give pleasure to men than I did. Aeram pulled me into the bed. "Come here, goddess." We finished the box of six chocolates in less than an hour.

James had told me he wanted me to redesign the house and I should look at things, but our lovemaking had taken up the better part of our stay there. Aeram even suggested we make love in a boat, but I chickened out of fear that our antics might capsize the boat. It was nice to just be ourselves. Nobody knew Aeram in Portugal. I suggested to him that we should use his birth-name, Aeram Ryan Albuquerque, to get good tables in restaurants but he refused. "I am my mother's son, Saysha. It's going to be Aeram Khan only."

The next day we took a long taxi ride to the Carmo Convent in Santa Maria Maior. Originally built in 1389, much of The Convent of Our Lady of Mount Carmel was broken in an earthquake in 1755. Of all the pretty sights and happy places Lisbon had to offer to tourists, my husband was determined to see only this one, located over an hour's drive away from our home in Alhandra. Standing under the pointed arches of the unroofed nave of the church, I asked him why. He looked at the pillars in awe and told me, "They survived, in spite of everything. Even an earthquake couldn't break them. They're like James." I was standing next to a man who was revered by millions of fans around the world, who worshipped only one person, his older brother, James Christian Albuquerque.

We watched the tourists while sipping our sangrias and having a meal of grilled fish and kale soup at a restaurant in Lisbon. Aeram wolfed down the pin-boned, filleted fish and asked for another grouper. He glanced at me and shrugged. "What? Why are you looking at me like that?"

"If you love fish so much, you must learn to debone it as well," I teased him.

He turned red from embarrassment. I sensed something was wrong. Then he chuckled, "No, I like the way James does it," and quickly changed the subject to his new movie. I pretended not to notice.

Later in the afternoon, we walked hand in hand along the Jardim Brás de Albuquerque, a beautiful garden in Alhandra, where sometimes young boys played soccer. We went past a cinema theatre when suddenly Aeram had an idea. We bought tickets and ran to our corner seats in the dark hall. We didn't watch even seconds of the Brazilian movie they were playing. It was as if we were in college in Delhi and had sneaked out to the cinema. I ran my fingers down my husband's gorgeous body. "I love you so much, Aeram." He gave me a long, deep kiss. We fondled and fingered each other and forgot every care in the world. It was us, just us.

As I lay in Aeram's arms that night, I thought about James and what he might be in for. The next morning, we were leaving for New York. James had specifically told me not to watch or read any news till we were back in India. I wondered why. The brothers were so alike. They held their cards close and revealed their hearts and secrets only to each other. They revolved around me but they lived for and because of each other.

PART 6

NEW YORK

Chapter 21

Sanam joined us directly in New York. I was looking forward to spending time with her. Even after a year into our marriage, I hadn't managed to form a relationship with her. She lived in her own world and seldom enquired about mine. She saw me only as her beloved brother's wife, just a distraction. I had hoped we would bond over shopping but our tastes were so different that we could not find anything to do together. She was seven years older than me but I had talked more with James who was nine years older. I yearned for him. He brought all of us together in this family.

The three of us were walking towards the Arrivals' gate of John F Kennedy International Airport when a tall blonde man with grey-green eyes came towards us holding a placard. It read, "AERAM KHAN." Aeram nodded and shook hands with him. He spoke with an American accent, "Hi, I am Igor. Monica is busy this week so I will be helping you out with everything you need."

"Thanks, Igor. This is my wife, Saysha."

Igor's eyes lingered on me a little longer than normal courtesy would allow.

He extended his hand and said, "Hi Saysha. Igor Lebedinsky. Pleased to meet you."

My eyes widened. Aeram noticed. He pointed to a group of Indian tourists coming towards us. "Let's leave or we'll be here forever. I am too tired to pose for selfies."

Our home for the next ten days was a spacious condominium on the thirtieth floor of Tower 58 on Manhattan's West 58th street. Aeram chose it because it was close to the offices of the representatives he wanted to visit and he did not want to sit in New York's notorious traffic jams for hours just to get to meetings.

The huge windows offered us a spectacular view of the city. The Times Square and Madison Avenue were a short walk away and so were all the theatres on Broadway. In the other direction, there was Central Park. On our way to the condominium, Sanam and I had made a note of all the boutiques and stores on the Fifth Avenue we had to visit. The only drawback was the traffic. Cars, taxis, buses, three-wheelers, bicycles, bikes and pedestrians vied for real estate dodging vendors, hustlers, beggars, muggers and buskers. People of every shape, size, colour, race, religion, sex and gender from everywhere in the world were there speaking zillions of languages.

Igor settled us in the apartment and left but not before giving me a curious glance. Aeram's muscles were stiff so he went to the gym. By the time he came back after an hour, all red and sweaty, I had changed into comfortable white cotton shorts and a white tank top and was looking inside the refrigerator for some food. "Hi," he said, panting. I took an ice cube out of the fridge and sucked it, seductively. He frowned. I ran it over his sweaty upper lip. It startled him. I sucked it again. "What the…" Before he could finish, I ran the ice-cube over his lips again and then put it in my mouth. He wanted more. He grabbed me and kissed me with the ice still in my mouth. Then he carried me straight into the shower. As we lay in bed, he whispered in my ear, "I love what you're watching and learning nowadays, Saysha." He kissed me on my lips. I thought of James. I ached for him. He had not responded to any of my texts since we had boarded the flight to Lisbon from Mumbai. I was worried.

Aeram stroked my hair and said, "What's the matter, Saysha?"

"I am thinking about James."

"Me too. You know he's not answering the damn phone," he sighed. A tear rolled down his cheek.

I sat upright. It was very unlike them to not communicate with each other.

"Even Manohar Uncle," Aeram added, "I just don't know what's going on."

I whipped out my phone and started googling news about 'Goa'.

Aeram put his hand on mine. "Don't. Not yet. It will only get us more worried. Let's wait till we get out of here. There's nothing we can do about it."

It was very unusual for my very rich and very powerful husband to admit defeat.

He stared at the ceiling and said, "Only James can go up against the might of Father Patrick and the church. It has to be his fight. If I get involved, there will be riots. I practise Islam, Saysha. Even if I don't show any symbols of my faith, the world knows that. I don't want blood on the streets for a property. Not in my name. Not in my mother's name. Not in Allah's name. We will wait and watch. Zarine from my PR team will help him if he needs her. So far, they have not communicated."

Chapter 22

We were having a breakfast of bagels and eggs when Igor walked in. He nodded to Aeram and Sanam and gave me a warm smile. I was curious to know if we were related in some way. After all, how many Lebedinskys could be there in Russia? Google didn't give too many answers though one caught my eye: Lebedinsky Mining was the largest producer of iron ore in Europe.

Igor was about my age. He worked in Monica Cohen's Talent Agency and was pursuing the Bachelor of Fine Arts at Lee Strasberg Theatre and Film Institute in New York. He hoped a day would come when Monica might represent him. He would have looked a lot more like me had he dyed his hair brown.

"Where are we going today, Igor?" Aeram asked.

"We have two meetings. One with Emma Watts's agent, Leo Davis, who will arrive from LA sometime now and we can discuss our schedules, shooting dates, etc. The second one is at a producer's office here in Manhattan. They are coming up with a short web-series and thought you might fit in because you're not the typical Indian actor."

I laughed. Igor's eyes crinkled when he smiled. Aeram shrugged, "I am still trying to figure what I am supposed to be. Great, Igor. Now, can you tell me how we can keep the ladies occupied while the two of us go to these meetings?"

Igor hesitated before answering. "Actually, Aeram, the producer wants you alone there and Emma Watts's agent will be meeting Monica and you at our office near Madison Square. I could look after the ladies while you're away."

"Sounds like a plan, Igor. They love shopping."

"They've come to the right place, Aeram." He smiled and left.

Sanam started her shopping spree at Saks Fifth Avenue. She tried on outfits and shoes while Igor waited for us patiently outside. After a splurge in Gucci, I was tired. Sanam was not. She fed off the adrenaline rush that came with trying out a new dress that fit her perfect body absolutely right. I, on the other hand, at a petite five-feet-three-inches realised that shopping in designer boutiques in the USA was quickly turning into an exercise of self-loathing. I joined Igor on the bench in the lobby while Sanam entered Louis Vuitton. He asked, "Coffee?" "That would be great." Igor left and came back after twenty minutes with Fika coffee cups. It was good but nowhere close to James's.

I started the conversation, "How long have you been in the US, Igor?"

He shrugged and said, "Well, I was born here, but my family is from Moscow so we lived there till I was six. We moved here for my school and have lived here ever since."

I smiled and enquired, "Are you anywhere related to the Lebedinsky Mining company?"

He chuckled. "My father owns it."

"What? Then why are you…"

"Working as an intern in a talent agency?" He completed the question that he must have been asked a million times. "Because I want my own identity. I want to be an actor."

I understood too well what living under an overachiever's shadow was like. Igor and I had something in common.

"You know my birth-mother was Russian." I felt like opening up to him.

He raised his eyebrows. "Really?"

"And the coincidence is that her name was Tatiana Lebedinsky. She shared your last name."

He turned red. I did not know how to continue the conversation so I looked away. Sanam came out carrying more shopping bags. "I think that's enough for today," she said. Igor chuckled.

We entered our apartment and found Aeram lounging on the couch in his black shorts and blue Nike vest, browsing his iPad. "How was your meeting, darling?" I gave him a peck on his cheek and asked him.

Aeram pulled me into his arms and replied, "It went well. I liked the idea of the web-series." He watched Igor struggle with our shopping bags and rose to help him. Taking a couple of bags in his hand, he turned to Sanam. "I hope you've left something for the other shoppers."

She whacked him on his shoulder and walked to her bedroom and shut the door behind her. Igor wondered where he should put the bags. Aeram put them on the dining table and Igor did the same.

"Do you need anything else?"

We shook our heads.

"Then, I'll see you tomorrow."

We waved him goodbye.

I turned to Aeram who was nibbling my earlobe and said, "His father owns Lebedinsky Mining."

"Really?" Aeram whispered and caressed my neck.

"But he wants to become an actor," I added, as Aeram moved his tongue up and down my neck and pretended to not pay attention.

"I mentioned Tatiana to him and he turned red," I added.

Aeram stopped and moved away from me. He shouted, "Saysha, why?"

I shrugged and told him, "It's a coincidence that he has the same name as my birth-mother."

"Saysha!" Aeram put his head in his hands and exclaimed. "Alexandre Lebedinsky is Tatiana and Svetlana Lebedinsky's older brother. Igor is your cousin."

What? Unbelievable! My husband knew and hadn't told me anything. The man got on my nerves!

Chapter 23

I wanted to learn more about Igor but Monica had reshuffled the duties of her staff and he was put in charge of a local actor who was trying to make the leap from stage to screen. I felt Aeram was responsible for the change but did not ask him. Instead, I tried to build a relationship with Sanam that did not involve retail therapy. Even someone as generous as Aeram had flipped when he saw the figures after a single day's shopping. To avoid another spree, I took Sanam to see the Statue of Liberty.

Sitting at Liberty's feet, we pointed at the skyscrapers in Manhattan and tried to identify them. A boy and a girl of about ten and eight were blowing bubbles at each other. Sanam watched them and said, "I miss James." We all did. He completed all of us in some way or the other. To Sanam he was more a brother than Aeram was. Aeram needed him to function as a normal being. He had said James was like oxygen to him. And I craved the love and attention he gave me. I hugged Sanam and she held me tight.

"Why don't you start your practice again?" I asked her. Sanam had stopped practising law since her mother's death. She looked at me as if I had asked her to visit the moon. I bit my lip. Then I remembered what James had told me about biting my lip. We didn't speak much through the rest of the trip.

Aeram was waiting for us when we got back to the apartment. Sanam went straight to her room. Aeram took me to the bed and started unbuttoning my shirt and kissing my neck. I grabbed his hair. After a dull outing with Sanam, I needed the thrill that came with sex. He was fingering me when his phone buzzed. He ignored it but it kept buzzing. He rose to take it. It was a message from James: Arriving tomorrow morning. Send the car to the airport.

Relief washed over him. A knot started to form in my stomach. I kissed him with a passion I had not felt in a while.

As we lay in each other's arms I told him about my visit with Sanam to the Statue of Liberty. "I don't know, Aeram, she just doesn't talk to me," I complained.

He kissed my forehead. "It's not like that. She likes you a lot but Sanam has always been very reserved. She was very attached to Marea and James. When Marea died after giving birth to me, she did not want to see my face because she thought I had killed her. She was only five and though she loves me a lot, somewhere at the back of her mind it still is there. We never really had the sibling relationship that James and she shared."

I could feel his pain. He loved his sister but she hardly returned his love. Aeram was a very lonely man. James and I were his universe. I realized how blessed I was to have a family where everyone had always been together and how Mom and Dad had given us a very normal and stable family.

Chapter 24

The energy and the mood of the room changed the moment James walked in through the door. First, Sanam ran to him and gave him the biggest hug and planted kisses on both his cheeks. Then, Aeram joined her and held him tight. And finally, he held me and kissed both my cheeks. Behind him stood Igor wondering what the fuss was all about. As Aeram and Sanam took James aside and asked him about news from Goa, I walked to Igor who smiled at me warmly.

"Hi, Igor."

"Hi Saysha."

"Looks like we are related, Igor," I said.

"Yeah, quite a surprise." He became a little uncomfortable.

James watched us with interest or maybe even a bit of envy. Igor was a handsome man.

I enquired, "How often do you go to Moscow?"

He shrugged. "Not much. The last time I went was five years ago to attend my grandmother's funeral."

Suddenly, I had an idea. "Hey, is there a nightclub around here where we can go?"

Igor smiled. "Of course! Will book tonight if you want."

"Thanks Igor."

"You're welcome," he nodded and left.

James stretched out on his bed. He patted the mattress next to him, "Come, sit with me, Saysha." I hesitated. He rolled his eyes, "Come on. I am asking you to sit with me, not have sex with me." I sat next to him and stretched my legs out. He put his head on my shoulder.

I asked him, "What happened in Goa?"

"I don't want to talk about that," he said and closed his eyes.

"Is it not over, yet?"

Without opening his eyes, he said, "No."

"Then why are you here?" I was curious.

"Because...", he sighed, "because I can't stay away from you." He kissed me lightly on my shoulder and put his arm around my lap.

I looked up and saw Aeram fuming at the door. His fists were clenched.

He shouted, "Saysha, what the hell are you doing in his room?"

James rolled his eyes and smirked. He sat upright.

Aeram was mad. He yelled at James, "What are you laughing for?"

I should have been scared but what came out of my mouth was, "Shut up, idiot!"

Colour left his cheeks.

"Come here," I beckoned him, "Sit with us!"

Aeram stood still. Then he shook his head and squeezed himself in between James and me and stretched out on the bed. James and I lay down too.

We gazed at the ceiling for a while and then Aeram started laughing. He turned towards James and lay on his side. He whispered, "Remember, you and I would lie like this in Marea's room when Papa wasn't in town and you would tell me ghost stories. I would get spooked and start crying. Then you would hold me tight and put me to sleep."

James was surprised and turned on his side towards Aeram. Their faces were just a few inches apart. He smiled and asked, "You remember that?"

Aeram sighed and turned and lay on his back. He stared at the ceiling and said, "Yes. We did that also when Danny wasn't in the house. We used to sneak into the room and look for Marea's things."

James stroked his head gently and asked, "How do you remember all that? You were just over five. Even the mirror thing at Marea's grave. I never thought you'd remember it, Aeram."

Still looking up, he replied, "I don't forget anything, James. I remember one time Danny dragged you into his room… and…" A tear rolled down Aeram's cheek. He sniffed and continued, "I saw what he did to you, James. I watched through the window and…"

James rolled on top of him and put a finger on his lips. "Stop, Aeram… please, stop." He caressed his cheek and wiped off the tears with his thumb. Then he rolled back onto the bed and sighed.

They were talking as if I wasn't there. I rose to leave them alone.

"Saysha, please stay with us," James pleaded.

I nodded and lay beside them. Aeram took my hand in his.

James spoke next: "You must forget some things, Aeram. It's not good for you to remember everything. It messes your head."

Aeram let out a sigh. "It helps with my acting. When the director wants me to do an intense scene or emote in a particular way, I recall those memories."

"It's not good to live those memories again and again, Aeram. Get a therapist. You've got the best for Sanam, why not one of them for yourself as well?"

Aeram scoffed. "And then the headline will read 'psycho superstar'. No thank you, you two are my best therapists."

James rolled his eyes. "Then talk to Saysha sometimes, instead of just having sex with her to drive away your pain or anxiety."

I turned red. They were talking as if I wasn't there lying next to the two of them.

Aeram tried to get up but couldn't. "Ouch!"

James frowned. "What happened, darling?"

"I've got this thing in my back since I arrived here. It's a catch or a spasm." Aeram winced.

James offered, "Need a massage?"

"Yes, please," Aeram begged him.

I interrupted them. "James is jet-lagged, Aeram. Let him rest." I got out of the bed but James was already removing his shirt and jacket. He went to the kitchen and brought some olive oil.

"Really James… you need to…" He put his finger on my lips.

"I don't get a chance to feel him up very often. He's got an awesome ass." He suggestively licked his lips and winked.

I squirmed.

"Don't tease her, James." Aeram glared at him. "I can't tolerate anyone teasing Saysha."

"Well, that makes two of us," James said very seriously. Then he threw a towel at Aeram. I left the room.

James entered my bedroom after half an hour. I was scrolling my Facebook newsfeed. "He has fallen off to sleep in my bed," he told me. I moved aside so James could lie down. He had worn only his soccer shorts. He kissed me on my cheek, held my hand and closed his eyes.

Chapter 25

When Monica Cohen walked into the apartment in her high Manolo Blahnik heels, we were all lounging in the living room. Aeram was scrolling his iPad, Sanam was editing her pictures on Instagram. I sat opposite James at the dining table. He had made coffee for all of us. The men were dressed identically in white shirts and blue jeans, the women in white summer dresses though it was autumn in New York. Monica wore a black pantsuit and a no-nonsense expression on her face. Her mouth was red and her curls were the colour of the autumnal orange maple leaves. She meant business. Igor followed her in a black suit and tie.

Aeram did a round of introductions as we gathered around her. She was taken in by James. "And do you want to be represented as well?" Her voice was husky.

James smiled. "No. I am his stuntman and I am happy doing just that." Aeram, Monica and Igor moved to the study to discuss the contract for the Hollywood film and the dates for the schedule. Sanam went into her room.

James and I sat quietly and sipped our coffees. I could see he had a lot going on in his head. He did not tell us anything about why he had suddenly come to New York. We were delighted he was with us but James would never tell us anything he did not want us to know. I reached for his hand. He kissed my palm, first lightly, then passionately. His eyes never left mine. I felt the butterflies in my stomach. Then, he let go of my hand and took a sip of his coffee. Aeram walked into the room with Monica and Igor after two minutes. James, in his deep sexy voice, asked Monica, "Want some coffee?" Her red lips quivered very slightly before she collected herself and said politely, "Not now but if you'd like to meet me later in the evening, I am free today."

"But Monica…" Igor interrupted, "you have to…"

Monica shot him a glance that shut his mouth. James replied, "Today's a busy day. Some other time. It was nice meeting you, Monica." He kissed her goodbye and headed to his room.

I was jealous.

Monica turned to Aeram and suggested, "We could work out a contract for him as well."

Aeram laughed. "I think he said no, Monica."

She shook her head and left, without saying goodbye to me.

James came out wearing his soccer shorts, Reebok vest and shoes. "I am going to hit the gym. Aeram, do you want to join me?" Aeram nodded and went to our room to change. James bent down and kissed my palm. "I'm yours." His voice was low and firm.

I traced the lines on my palm and smiled to myself.

Later in the evening, Aeram had to go as chief guest to a pre-Diwali bash conducted by the Indian Association of Brooklyn. One of his film's financiers was organising it. The press would be there in full attendance. James, Sanam and I decided to skip it. Then Sanam found an old friend through Facebook and made plans for dinner with her leaving James and me alone.

I was lounging on the sofa, when James asked me if I wanted to go out for dinner somewhere. I had never gone out alone for a meal with him so I hesitated. "Come on, I am hungry," he said, suggestively. I blushed and agreed. Dressed casually in jeans, t-shirts, jackets and sneakers, we walked down the street to Madison Square Garden. Kebab, churro and ice-cream stalls lined the thoroughfare. We found a small Chinese takeaway tucked in Broadway Street that catered to the crowd that was waiting to enter one of the theatres to watch *Hamilton*. I noticed how comfortable James was in New York. He wandered through the streets as if he walked them every other day.

He ordered the takeaway; noodles, crispy pork belly and a couple of cans of Coke. We found seats in Madison Square Garden where some of New York's rock-heads were to perform. It was a free-for-all. We tucked into our noodles with chopsticks. After a struggle, I finally managed to lift some to put into my mouth when James opened his and slurped it up, dribbling sauce all over his chin. He laughed and dabbed his chin with a napkin. I scowled at him. He laughed even more. I punched him.

"Ow, Saysha." He then deftly picked up some noodles from his cup and put it in my mouth. This was the first time we had shared a meal. It seemed like the most normal thing for us to do.

We were walking back to the apartment holding hands, when I asked him, "James, when did you fall in love with me?"

"The first time I saw you," he replied without looking at me.

I asked, "When you drove us back to Delhi from Shimla?"

He shook his head. "No, when you arrived at the cottage from the prom and I left the pizzas for you on the kitchen counter."

I was surprised. "But we didn't see you."

He smiled and looked at me. "I did. I was walking out when you guys arrived. You were making out in the car. I just glanced backwards when he opened the door and helped you out. The moon shone on your face. God! You looked so beautiful, Saysha."

I started getting goosebumps. He held me by my waist and pulled me close to him. "I had never felt like that for a girl before. Hell, actually, I had never felt like that for anybody before, man or woman, so I talked myself out of it at night and thought it was just a passing thing till Aeram introduced us the next morning. The memory of the previous night came back. Then I caught you checking me out in the mirror a few times during that long drive." He chuckled. I blushed. He stopped walking and kissed me on my cheek. His lips just inches away from mine. I wanted him so badly. "You don't know how many times I have tried to talk myself out of this. We cannot be in a relationship. We cannot call this friendship. I don't know what this is other than the fact that I am madly in love with you and you are madly in love with me, Saysha."

"I am crazy about you, James," I whispered and tried to kiss him. He tilted his head and it landed as a peck on his cheek.

PART 7

MUMBAI

Chapter 26

We returned to India after two weeks to discover that Goa was all over prime-time TV news. Sanam had flown straight to Delhi and James had left four days earlier for Goa. We walked to the Arrivals' section of the Chhatrapati Shivaji International Airport in Mumbai and waited for Zarine's car to pick us up. I glanced at the ticker on TV:

Church sex scandal: Will Goa Archbishop Patrick Mascarenhas step down?

What? I tried to get a closer look at the screen but Aeram pulled me away towards Zarine's waiting car.

She smiled at us and drove us away from the paparazzi in her Hyundai i20 while our bags followed in Aeram's Audi. A couple of photographers had figured the decoy and given us chase but most were confused.

Zarine dropped me home and took Aeram to her house in Tardeo where the entire PR team were meeting. It was not even 4 am.

Tired after the flight, I just crashed into my bed, unaware of the tornado that was going to hit us the next morning. When I woke up well past noon, I groggily asked the cleaner if Aeram was back. She said no. I asked her to make some coffee since James wasn't around and plonked myself on a chair at the dining table. The coffee was weak and I needed a second cup before picking up the newspaper. The headline read:

"Aeram's stunt-double alleges Goa Archbishop raped him as a child"

I spat out the coffee and started coughing. The cleaner was apologetic. I waved her away, briskly, and read the rest of the story:

Panjim: In a shocking revelation, superstar Aeram Khan's stuntman, James Albuquerque, has alleged that Father Patrick Mascarenhas, the newly appointed Archbishop of Goa and Daman, had raped him as a child. The news comes at a time when the Vatican has been accused of covering up child sexual abuse cases globally.

In an FIR filed at the Mapusa police station, Albuquerque, who is now 32, has alleged that Father Patrick and his accomplices raped him from the age of 12 to 15 years, when he was a student at a missionary boarding school in Mapusa. Two other former students of the same school have also filed FIRs against Father Patrick and the school. Both are in their thirties. They have alleged that the school was an institution of abuse, torture and corruption. The police have sealed the school's premises.

Father Patrick had taken office at The Sé Catedral de Santa Catarina in Old Goa just last month. However, in the face of such serious allegations there have been calls for him to step down till the investigations are completed. James Albuquerque was not available for comment.

I switched on the TV and found the story on every news channel. James Albuquerque was touted as the David who was to take down the Goliath, Father Patrick. He was nowhere to be seen. A few journalists had tried to get Aeram to say something on the issue but all he offered was, "It's not my matter to comment on." But where the hell was James?

Aeram finally walked in at 4 pm, fourteen hours after we had landed in Mumbai. He was exhausted. I fixed his bath. "Saysha, please join me," he sighed and stretched out his hand. He put his head on my shoulder. I asked, "Where is James?"

Aeram shook his head. "All I know is he isn't in India. He didn't take the flight back here?"

"What?" I was worried. "Where can he be?" Aeram held his head in his hands. He stayed like that for minutes.

Then he started laughing.

I thought he had gone mad after losing James.

His eyes twinkled.

I demanded, "Why are you laughing? Your brother's nowhere to be found. Everyone from the media, the cops and the church are looking for him. And you're laughing? Are you insane?"

Then he looked at me and said softly, "Think of the one place you will go to if you want to escape from everything and everyone, where no one knows you, to which no one knows you're connected, where you're in a home away from home."

I frowned. Then it hit me. James was in Alhandra, Portugal. He would wait it out until Father Patrick was forced to resign and going by the Vatican's new policy regarding child sexual abuse, that seemed like a possibility soon. The Catholic Church could not afford to be more embarrassed than they already were. Aeram grinned.

Chapter 27

It had been a week since our return to India from the US, since James's explosive revelations shook the entire institution of the Catholic Church in India. We had figured where he might be but couldn't reach him. I missed him, more, because Aeram was busy working on a new web series. I was alone in the house trying to finish a couple of jobs Neelam had set aside for me when my phone buzzed.

It was a message from Rachel: Wanna meet?

Saysha: Sure

Rachel: Starbucks, Horniman Circle?

Saysha: Ok

In James's absence, Aeram had asked one of his drivers from office to help me get around the city but I chose a taxi like the last time I had gone for a coffee with Rachel.

We were sipping our lattes when Rachel told me the news: "Lionel and I broke up."

"Why? When?"

She shrugged, "Well he wasn't here much and I found someone better."

My eyes widened. "Really? Who?"

"Cyrus. He's on Aeram's tech team. You must have seen us dancing at your anniversary bash."

Of course, I did! I was trying to avoid being seen while dancing with James.

"Well, he's kind of cute," Rachel added.

"I am happy for you, Rachel. But how did Lionel take it?"

"He was cool, Saysha. I think he knew it was coming. Besides, he had also had a couple of flings on the side in Rio de Janeiro."

That was astonishing. "How can you be so cool about it, Rachel?"

She giggled and used her right hand to swat an imaginary fly. "Not everyone is made for monogamy like you and Aeram."

Then she batted her eyelashes and asked, "By the way, how is loverboy?"

I blushed. "He has gone for a script session for his new web series."

She slapped my arm. "*Arre*, not Aeram. I am talking about James."

I turned red and shook my head. "No idea. Haven't seen him since we got back from the US."

"That man has balls to take on Father Patrick of all people. Even my dad would think twice. And he is a Kargil hero!"

I agreed. James had more character than most men.

My phone buzzed. It was Aeram.

He asked softly, "Where are you, Saysha?"

"Colaba," I said, "With Rachel."

I heard him exhale. Then he said, "James is coming to pick you up. Wait at Regal. He's driving the Audi."

What? My heart skipped a few beats.

Rachel looked concerned. "Is everything okay?"

"I've got to go to Regal, Rachel. I'll see you another time."

"Should I come along?"

"No." I was almost running.

I wanted to be alone with James before anyone else saw or met him.

The Audi barely stopped for seconds before I jumped into the backseat.

James looked at me in the rear-view mirror and smiled. I returned it. We drove in silence to Worli.

Only after we were safely in our house, did I dare to hug him. He held me tight and then he started kissing me all over my face except my lips. I tried to break his hold to take a breather but he didn't let me go. He ran his tongue over my collarbones and kissed me on my neck. Finally, he released me.

"I have missed you Saysha. I love you so much," he said and took me in his arms again and started kissing my neck.

"When did you come back, James?" I finally managed to ask him.

"Right now. Came straight from the airport to pick you up. Aeram's coming here." He held me tight and kissed me on my cheeks. Then he picked me up, took me to the patio and sat me down on a sofa. He took off his blazer, kicked off his shoes and rested his head on my shoulder. He whispered the words from the EE Cummings's poem:

I fear no fate for you are my fate, my sweet

I want no world for beautiful you are my world, my true

His fingers traced my collarbones. A knot started to form in my stomach. He kissed the length of my neck and then licked my earlobes. I grabbed his collar tight. Then he kissed me on my cheek and sat on the other sofa, while I gasped for breath. Aeram walked in after five minutes. He kissed me on my cheek and then went on to hug James.

Chapter 28

James switched on the TV. Father Patrick had announced a press conference to refute all the allegations James and the other two complainants had made. "He will rip me apart in public," James chuckled. My nerves were getting to me. Taking on the might of the Church wasn't the best move forward. Already, Father Patrick's supporters were clamouring for James's blood. There was this whole section of conservatives who joked about his sexuality and orientation. There were memes, trolls and fake videos, which James knew nothing about because he had never been on social media.

"How can you be so cool, James?"

He said coldly, "I have nothing more to lose. Whatever I had to lose, I lost when I was twelve. I'll make him pay."

Father Patrick appeared on screen. For a man in his late seventies, he looked extremely fit. He was tall like Aeram, clean shaven with white hair that looked like feathery clouds. Icy blue eyes stood out against his wheatish complexion. A chill ran down my spine.

He bellowed:

"There have been some very serious allegations levelled against me and this great Catholic institution by a certain individual who calls himself James Albuquerque but is neither an Albuquerque, nor Catholic. He was the adopted son of a housekeeper at Albuquerque near Old Goa, of a woman known only by her first name because she kept more than one man in her life."

James turned red with rage. His fists were clenched.

Father Patrick continued, "Imagine an individual, whose whereabouts are not known, whose family is nowhere, who has no respect for the scriptures and has committed a detestable sin by keeping relations with other men, claims that the person who holds the highest office in the church..."

Before he could finish, there seemed to be a commotion in the audience. Father Patrick looked in that direction. A couple of priests whispered in his left ear. His expression changed suddenly. He grabbed the microphone and in a voice that was struggling to remain calm, said, "There is a matter I need to attend to urgently. I will take your leave now. The Archdiocese will send a press release to all of you later. Thank you."

James laughed. I was confused. He switched off the TV, turned around and hugged me. Aeram, who had been sitting with his technical team in the study downstairs, walked in with a big grin on his face. "Done!" He shouted and hugged James.

I had to ask, "What is done?"

Then Aeram showed me a video on WhatsApp. It showed Father Patrick with two little boys at the missionary school in Mapusa. The boys seemed drugged. They were sitting on Father Patrick's lap. The next part of the clip showed Father Patrick in a room with the same boys. It looked like one of the dorm rooms meant for the prefect or warden. The third part was way too graphic and stomach-churning. I felt for the boys and started crying.

"We had to get the horny bastard," Aeram shouted.

I asked, "How did this get filmed?"

Aeram replied, "Well, it seems not everyone at the school were okay with Father Patrick's antics. A couple of teachers had filmed these on different occasions but they were too meek to do anything. James tracked them down and guaranteed them complete anonymity. My tech team did the editing and we released it right now, when Father Patrick was going to mention the Albuquerque property clause. It would have done us a lot of damage if Xavier's clause became public. This has already gone viral. Denial will be difficult. Patrick Mascarenhas will have to resign."

One after another, the news channels carried the story of the video. By 9 pm, the Archdiocese announced that Father Patrick had resigned and the police were investigating the case after taking the former Archbishop into custody. Father John Rodericks from Ponda would take over the office till a new Archbishop was appointed.

"You're brilliant," I hugged Aeram and kissed him.

He kissed me back and said, "That I am, but James is a genius."

I looked from one to another.

"James?"

He nodded. "It was his plan. It always is."

James smiled and winked at me.

I felt as if I didn't know him at all.

Chapter 29

Aeram left for Delhi early in the morning to meet with Sanam and my parents and then travel to Chandigarh for a string of events that ranged from a book launch to a store opening to an exhibition cricket match. He would be gone for two days. James went to drop him at the airport. I sat on the patio watching the sea as dawn slowly broke and the first fishermen and women brought in their tiny boats with their first catch of the day. The salt spray of the ocean and the cool breeze caressed my face. I stood at the edge of the patio next to the wall and felt as if I was sailing in a ship. I closed my eyes. A familiar hand caressed my cheek. I opened my eyes to find James. He licked my cheek.

"Eww James, you're so gross," I told him and tried to move away.

He pinned me to the wall and licked my face, neck and shoulders. My body was on fire and my nails dug into his back. He picked me up and took me to his room and put me on his bed. The sheets smelled of peppermint. I was madly in love with him. If he had wanted, I would have given him sex at that instant. But he did not want me for sex. He had men for that.

He lay down next to me and stroked my hair. "I love you, Saysha." "I love you, James." I tried to kiss him. He moved away. Since that day in Goa when we both had kissed months ago, he had never let me kiss him, maybe a peck or two on the cheek, but nothing more.

He took off his Cross and put it around my neck. I had touched it only once before. I hadn't realised how heavy the chunk of solid 24 carat gold embedded with rubies, pearls and sapphires was. It was the size of a Marie biscuit. Right in the centre of the Cross was another enamelled cross-like structure that James told me was Portugal's sea flag of the 1500s. The white in the centre was mother-of-pearl dotted with tiny blue sapphires. Afonso de Albuquerque had worn it for all his voyages to conquer the spice trade from the Arabs. He had given it to his bastard son, Manuel, to maintain his name and legacy in India. I felt the weight of its history around my neck. James had strutted around wearing it as if he had picked it up from one of those fake antique shops along Colaba Causeway.

I was so busy admiring the pendant that I didn't notice when he had left the room. He came back with my sketchbook and colour pencils. He lay me down on the pillows and sat opposite me to sketch. I felt like Rose from the film, *Titanic*. The only difference was that I was clothed in black shorts and white t-shirt.

"Why are you smiling?" James asked me without looking up.

"This reminds me of the scene from *Titanic*."

Dimples formed on his cheeks. He looked into my eyes and in a deep sexy voice he asked, "Do you want me to make your nudes?"

I turned red.

He laughed. "Great! Blush looks good in sketches."

I blushed more.

After a few minutes of silence, while he furiously sketched my outline, I asked, "Why don't you let me kiss you, James?"

He put the pencil down and caressed my cheek. "Because you promised him that you won't kiss me and I don't want you to break that promise. I can't see him hurt like that."

"I never thought I was capable of loving two people at the same time, James."

He went back to his drawing. "We don't know what we're capable of Saysha. Till a year ago, I wouldn't have dreamt of taking on Father Patrick alone, forget about fighting the whole Church. And yesterday…"

"Then where did you find the strength?"

He looked at me and replied, "Because of his love and yours. Two people who love me the most in the world were standing behind me. That gave courage to the man who had to pretend he was the adopted son of his own parents and half-brother to his own siblings. Love is a powerful emotion, Saysha."

We remained quiet for a while. Then he turned the sketch towards me. The colour pencil sketch looked almost like a photograph. He was brilliant!

"Thank you," I said. My eyes were brimming with tears.

He kissed me on my forehead and led me out of the room.

Chapter 30

Since Aeram wasn't around, James and I decided to go to a restaurant for dinner, not one of those fancy fine-dining places we were forced to go to with Aeram because of his celebrity status, but a typical middle-class Chinese food joint at Fort, Five Spice. We waited for our table like everybody else. It was Saturday night. The place was full. I noticed the college girls were ogling at James. He looked dapper in his white shirt and blue jeans. The top three buttons were undone to reveal his muscled chest. He hadn't worn the Cross. A couple of men were staring at me. I had worn a strappy denim mini-dress and brown wedges. I was standing with my back towards them when one of them brushed against me. I moved closer to James. Since I hadn't responded to the man in any way, his friend got bolder and placed his hand on my back. I squirmed and moved even closer to James. Two seconds later, the man lay wincing on the floor, with his hands between his legs. James wrapped me in his arms and kissed my forehead.

As we sat down and stared at the menu, a familiar voice called my name out. It was Rachel. She was there with Cyrus and a couple of other friends. She came to our table. James didn't look up from the menu. His expression was blank.

"Hi Saysha. What a surprise!" She gave me a hug. I became aware that people had started looking in my direction. My name was unusual and most people associated it with a very popular unusual name, Aeram. Rachel didn't care. She turned to James and in her singsong voice greeted him, "Hi James."

He replied cordially, "Hi Rachel," and went back to the menu.

Before she could hold a conversation with him, he called the waiter and ordered Hakka noodles, kung pao potatoes and chicken in black bean sauce. Then he looked at me and asked, "Anything else?"

I shook my head. I was aware that people were trying to figure who we were. Finally, Rachel got the hint and left us alone.

My phone beeped. It was a message from her: What are you doing with him?

I replied: Wanted to have a quiet dinner at a non-fancy place, that's it. Don't yell my name out in public, please. Everyone is staring at me.

Rachel responded: I am so sorry Saysha. I didn't realize. Enjoy your dinner. See ya later.

The food arrived at our table. We ate in silence. Sauce dribbled down my chin. James reached for a tissue and dabbed it. While he did that, he slid his thumb between my lips and winked at me. Then craftily, he threw the tissue away with his other hand and sucked his thumb. No one would have noticed. The memory of my second day in college flashed through my head, when I had wiped sauce off Aeram's lips during our first lunch together.

Intermittently, I caught Rachel watching us from her table a few times. James and I didn't talk much. The portions were large and we ate slowly. Finally, when we were done, I rose and went to Rachel's table to say goodbye. James paid the bill and waited outside the restaurant. Rachel and I walked out together. Cyrus was settling their accounts with the manager. James smiled at her. She smiled back.

"James, you are a real-life hero," she said proudly. He smiled. "Man, really to take on Father Patrick…"

"Not here, Rachel, please," he didn't let her finish.

"Sure. Come over sometime. Instead of just waiting for her in the car after you drop her at my place." She looked at me. I avoided looking at her.

James laughed. "I will. See you."

He held me close with one hand on my waist as we walked towards the car that he had parked in the next lane. Rachel was watching us. James didn't care. He kissed me on my forehead.

He was silent while driving down Marine Drive as I watched the streetlights cast shadows on his beautiful face.

My phone buzzed. It was Rachel.

"You two looked like you're very much in love."

I didn't reply.

As soon as we reached home, James kissed me on my face, neck and shoulders. I wanted to kiss him back but he didn't let me. He covered my lips with his fingers and continued to kiss me all over my body. It was a strange sensation. I wanted to go all out but couldn't. Then he let go of me and whispered, "Coffee?"

I nodded.

We sat across each other staring at our coffee mugs for a while.

Finally, I started the conversation I wanted to have with him.

"James, what happened in Goa when we left for Alhandra and New York?"

He smacked his lips and looked away. He was thinking hard, trying to collect all his thoughts to put them into words.

I stretched out my hand to hold his. "Please tell me."

He raised my hand to his lips and kissed it. Holding it with both his hands, he told me:

"The first two days, there was nothing. You were in Alhandra and I missed you like crazy. I moved out of the Albuquerque property into Manohar *mama's* house in Panjim. They used to live in Mapusa earlier but now they prefer Panjim where his practice is. Then, the day you landed in New York and Zarine publicised it in the papers, I got a call from Danny's lawyer to visit him in the office. I took Manohar *mama* along. He had known Albert Vaz since his law college days. They were friends outside of court. Albert alerted us to what Father Patrick had in mind following Danny's tragic death in the accident. I wish he wasn't drunk that day. It was a simple manoeuvre that cost him his life. He could have saved himself even after crashing into my car. Albert suggested we go to Sé Catedral in Old Goa and talk to Father Patrick and come to a settlement behind closed doors without anyone knowing anything about it. That was the best way forward, he believed. And I believed him. This was on Saturday so we fixed an appointment for Monday and it was given to us very easily. I was actually surprised how smoothly everything went.

"On Sunday, I attended the Mass at the Immaculate Conception Church in Panjim. That's when I figured something was wrong. Instead of Father Ribeiro, Archbishop Patrick stood at the pulpit. It was unexpected. Luckily, I was at the back somewhere so he couldn't see me. When he started his passionate sermon, I realized that in spite of his advanced years, the man had not changed one bit. His tirade was against the north Indian labourers who were coming to work in Goa's mines and construction businesses, some even took on local Catholic names so that they could get jobs. He went on and on about the repercussions of having non-Catholics coming in droves and ruining the fabric of society. And then without naming her, he mentioned my mother as 'a woman of Anglo-Indian origin of no great connections, probably born of sin herself, who had corrupted the mind of a very vulnerable mild young man belonging to one of Goa's most powerful and oldest Portuguese families. They lived in sin through their lives and had a bastard child who has laid claim on such a historic piece of land. Should we allow this again and again? Are we not good Catholics?' I had to use all my willpower to keep my butt on the bench. There was no point in meeting him. He would only find ways to hurt me more. I decided to fly to New York to join you guys. That evening, I visited the estate and then Manohar *mama* and I drove to Mapusa police station to file the FIR against Father Patrick. I flew to Mumbai and then to New York that night, first class."

I smiled. He pressed my hand and then continued:

"Over the last two months, since Danny decided to contest the wills in court, Aeram and I had worked out that the best way to keep them out of the property would be to put them in jail for their most sinister deeds. Danny figured I was investigating his past and tried to get rid of me. When I was in hospital after the accident, my roommate was a man who was injured in a brawl in one of the beach shacks around Calangute. He turned out to be a junior from my school in Mapusa. I was known as a soccer player, used to be the centre-forward, and then had become infamous for being kicked out of school because I was gay. We started talking and he broke down and told me about how Father Patrick and his friends had abused him for three years whenever Father Patrick visited the school, which was usually four to six times a year. He got the courage to file an FIR after my FIR became public. And then there was another student as well. That gave me credibility because mine wasn't the only case. The cops took their own time to make things public because of the name involved. But when the first report came out in the *Panjim Pioneer*, Zarine took over and made it known to the entire Mumbai press. This happened when we were in New York. You know what followed next. I feared retaliation from the Church so I decided to camp in Alhandra for a few days. Nobody knows of our property there. No one knows us there. It's the best place to keep a low profile."

I nodded. My mad husband had figured it out. James kissed my hand.

"Thankfully, because of the Vatican's new policy dealing with child sex abuse cases, I didn't have to hide for too long."

He took a sip of his coffee. We remained silent for a few minutes. It seemed like he was composing himself for what he was going to disclose next. Slowly, he said,

"Marea Williams was not low-born, Saysha. She was not born out of sin. Her father, Dr Albert Williams was an Englishman of high-birth and her mother, Georgina, was born in an Anglo-Indian family that ran a cloth business in Bombay. She went to the best girls' schools there. Georgina and Marea fell on hard times only after Dr Albert died of malaria in the jungles of south Gujarat where he was treating tribes for dysentery. Georgina worked as seamstress first but a governess's job paid more. After India got its Independence from the British, the Goan Portuguese elite realized that they might fare better if their children learned English too instead of just Portuguese so keeping English or Anglo-Indian governesses and nannies became a matter of prestige in Goa."

A thought crossed my mind. "I wonder why Father Patrick hates Marea so much."

James answered without looking up from his coffee. "Because she turned him down, that's why." He ran his left hand through his long brown hair. "Mamma loved Papa since they were children. But Mamma was renowned for her beauty. Many boys in the neighbourhood wanted her. Brother Patrick was one of them. He was madly in love with her even before she actually hit her teens."

I was shocked. "How do you know all this?"

James replied, "After I got kicked out of school, I had many questions about myself, my identity, what I should do, where I should go, etc. After making some money working in the farms, I visited Vasco where my *nana*, my grandmother, Georgina, lived with her brother, Joseph. They asked me to stay with them but I had already signed myself as a farm hand near Albuquerque and didn't want to stay anywhere but at Mamma's house. I knew Farah would come there to look for me. I visited my grandmother from time to time till she died four years ago. I took Aeram to meet her when he had come to visit the property after he turned twenty-one. That was the last time I saw her. Over the years, little by little, I pieced together the story of my family. Now, we're piecing together our family, Sanam, Aeram, you and me."

I wondered if the brothers meeting each other after fifteen years was a matter of chance or fate. "What if Aeram had not come to Mumbai looking for you?"

He grinned. "I would have gone to their house in Delhi. I knew where they lived. Manohar *mama* and Farah were always in touch with each other."

I was curious. "Then why didn't you go earlier?"

James's cheeks turned red with embarrassment. "Because I was angry that Farah had left only me behind. I was twelve. I sort of blamed her for what happened to me in the school in Mapusa. I believed that if I had gone to Delhi with them, none of that would have happened. I disliked her until the moment Aeram walked in through the door of my flat in Mumbai. I have loved him since the day he was born and had never stopped loving him. When he told me about his maths teacher in school and Feroz, I felt his pain and realized that Farah wasn't the problem. I wish I was there to protect him."

I raised my eyebrows. "Aeram told you all that during your first meeting? He told me only now, one year into our marriage, and four years since we met." My husband was weird.

James smiled. "It was as if he was waiting all those years to tell me everything. Richard was a distant father to him because Aeram reminded him of Mamma's death and he had lapsed into depression and then cancer. Sanam never warmed to him because Marea had died after giving him birth and she was very close to Marea. Farah was too busy working to make ends meet and fighting off lawsuits that Richard's distant cousins kept filing in courts to get their hands on Albuquerque properties. Ibrahim didn't like Aeram because Feroz was forced to go to America after Farah discovered he had sexually abused her beloved son." James's jaw was tight. He shook his head and shouted as if he were in pain, "Nobody heard him out. Nobody understood him and his pain. He doesn't trust anybody, Saysha. Too much was taken away from him too soon. He became the man of the house when he was only fifteen. He had to show the world how strong he was, while something kept breaking inside him."

I bit my lip. James frowned and then lowered his voice. "You remember, the three of us were lying on the bed in New York?" I nodded. "You wanted to leave because the conversation did not involve you and I told you to stay. He doesn't bare his soul to anyone but me, Saysha. I wanted you to have a peek into it. He has a lot of problems that he will never admit to anyone but me. He knows he can be vulnerable and cry his heart out when he's with me. The day he told you how he was abused by Feroz and his maths teacher and bullied by his friends, he was talking to you but thinking that he was talking to me with his eyes closed. I know you figured that out and allowed me into your room for the same reason. Thank you, Saysha. Not many spouses understand the kind of trust and love brothers have. And to keep that level of trust, I tell him everything. If we kiss, he will know because I will tell him even if he's crushed by the revelation."

I smirked. "He didn't know where I got the ice-cube and chocolate tricks from?"

James snorted and said, "Okay, well not everything. But he enjoyed them, didn't he?"

I nodded. James laughed. Then he became serious again. "He knows how much I love you, Saysha, and he knows he can't love you the way I love you. He can't give as much of himself to you as I do. But having said that, he is the most generous soul on earth and he is crazy about you."

I smiled. My phone buzzed. It was a text from Aeram: I love you baby. Miss you so much. Can we do video calling please?

I looked up from the phone. James shut the door of his bedroom.

Chapter 31

After months of going back-and-forth between the producer, director, screenplay-writer and actors, finally the bound script of the period film landed on Shweta's table. We had something concrete to work with. The working title of the movie was *Darbaar*, though everyone knew that there had to be a change in the name before it hit the screens. The director had suggested we erect the sets in Karjat, where most of the shoot would take place. His idea was to create a mini-town there where the entire crew would camp for a month-and-a-half and he would shoot two-thirds of the film. The rest one-third was to be shot in Rajasthan, Delhi, Agra and Fatehpur Sikri.

There was excitement all around the office. My days got busier and longer. Neelam and I visited all kinds of stores in the streets around Crawford Market to buy materials for props. We visited the market in Sewri to order the wood for our sets and walked through the narrow bylanes of Dharavi to find craftsmen who could execute our work. Then there were huge swathes of fabric that needed to be bought, for which we scrounged the markets of Musafirkhana, Sion and Parla. James accompanied me. The man had the smarts to drive a bargain where there was none. Aeram was busy with his shoots and readings for his first Hollywood film that he would start shooting in the US in December.

I was busy listing inventory for the shoot when Aeram walked in. It was late. James had gone out to meet some friends. Aeram bent down and kissed my lips. Then he loosened my hair from the ponytail and ran his fingers through it. We hadn't really spent much time with each other over the last couple of weeks because we were so busy. "Are you liking the job, Saysha?" He whispered. "Yes," I replied. He started unbuttoning my shirt as I tried to concentrate on the spreadsheet in front of me. "I need sex," he whispered and pressed my earlobe with his lips. I kissed him. He opened my shirt and kissed me down my chest as I pulled out his t-shirt. We were in the middle of a makeout session when James walked in. He saw us and walked out of the apartment.

Chapter 32

Diwali was a busy time for the Indian film industry, when all the big producers sought to release their films to get the lion's share of the audience that were willing to splurge after getting their bonuses and make the most of the school and college holidays. Naturally, we were busy. The entire week was booked for pujas, premieres, previews, card parties, cocktails, birthday bashes and Diwali parties. Since all the events through the week were going to be public and garner a lot of press, Zarine suggested I get a stylist and plan my outfits in advance. Tanvi Joshi had worked with many young actresses and star-wives who had managed to transform their awkward selves into Instagram goddesses. I didn't want that kind of following. My Instagram followers still were less than two thousand and I was content. Aeram's was more than two million. But Tanvi was adamant that I should work on my public persona and so I had meetings with designers. I still steered clear of Sabyasachi. After days of sifting through design, catalogues and outfits, I finally picked three designers for the Diwali week: Shantanu and Nikhil, Falguni and Shane Peacock and Masaba.

The first event of the week was Shan's cocktail party. I was in no mood to join the snob club there but Aeram insisted that both James and I had to go and added the clause that we had to stay there through the party. He was still mad at us for leaving him alone during Shan's birthday bash and going off on our own for a walk by the sea.

The invite said, "Desi girl/boy." I did not know what that meant. Tanvi said that it was the dress code and so I would have to channel my inner Priyanka Chopra. She picked a dark blue one-shoulder saree-gown for me, with diamonds to complement it and suggested I do up my hair in a tight bun to show off my neck and face. The outfit, hair and makeup took three hours to put together. I envied the two men who just threw on a black shirt and silver-grey suit, half-combed their hair, slipped their feet into shiny black brogues and were ready in half an hour for the party of the season, while I had to plan my pee-breaks. James would have worn shorts, vest and slippers just to get under fashion-obsessed Shan's skin but Aeram would have none of it and dressed him in Ermenegildo Zegna. To keep up with Shan's theme, Aeram wore a studded mango-motif diamond brooch on his coat's breast pocket. James sniggered.

Shan hugged Aeram tight as soon as he saw us. He kissed me on both my cheeks, ran a hand down my back and nodded a hello to James. Then he led us to his lawn where the party was in full swing. Everyone posed for pictures for the press photographers who were invited and the paparazzi outside who were not. People who bitched about each other, couldn't stand each other, were jealous of each other, came together in duck-face selfies. I got pulled into one of them by Tia. James found Joe and they walked towards the bar. He turned around, caught my eye and mouthed the words, "Call me," gesturing with his right hand. Shan took Aeram inside where Imran, Sangha, Ravi and he were playing cards. After sometime, he joined Tia and me while we were posing for selfies. "Hello, ladies, give me a kiss, come on," he squealed and put his arms around the two of us. Tia gave him a peck on the cheek in the light of the flashbulbs. Then he pointed to his cheek and looked at me. "Come on, Saysha, give me a kiss." I didn't move. "Oh! Come on," he said and caressed my cheek with his hand. I squirmed.

"Don't tease her, Shan." It was James's voice. Shan dropped his hand and turned around. James was standing ten paces away and fuming. From behind him, Aeram was walking towards us. He put a hand on James's shoulder as if to calm his down and continued in my direction. I could see he was mad at Shan. "Don't ever do that again, Shan," Aeram hissed. Then he held me tight as we walked away. The cameras kept clicking. He stopped near James, who was still glaring at Shan and whispered, "Take Saysha home. I'll ask Imran to drop me." He then turned to me and kissed me on my lips in front of everyone and escorted James and me out. Shan apologized. "I am so sorry, Saysha. I was just having fun. Don't leave the party." But I was already in the backseat of the Audi. Aeram turned to Shan. "I'm staying. That should be enough."

We were quiet while James drove through the Worli-Bandra Sealink. His knuckles were white from gripping the wheel too tight. My throat was parched. "James, can we just go ahead to Haji Ali Juice Centre? I need something to drink," I requested him.

He nodded.

When he stopped the car and asked me what I wanted to order, I pleaded, "Can we get out and walk? The weather is nice."

He looked around and shook his head. "Not here, Saysha. Not when we are dressed like this. Which juice do you want?"

I ordered a Ganga Jamuna, a mocktail of orange and sweet lime juice. He didn't get anything for himself. I sipped the juice in the car while we drove home.

As soon as we closed the door of the apartment, he held me tight and kissed me on my lips with so much passion that my body just melted away. He let me kiss him and I kissed him all over, his lips, his face, his neck, his chest. When we broke away for breath, he put his forehead to mine. "I didn't know what I was missing, Saysha," he whispered and kissed me again. When we finally let go of each other, I begged him, "Please don't tell Aeram about this. Please."

James bit his lip so hard that it started to bleed.

"Please," I implored him.

"Ok," he promised.

I went to the bathroom to get a ball of cotton and water.

As I dabbed his lip he held my hand, looked into my eyes and said, "I love you, Saysha."

"I love you, James."

Aeram stumbled in the darkness of our bedroom sometime early in the morning. I heard him rip his clothes off and slide into the bed next to me.

I woke up late in the morning. The sun streamed in through the blinds, lighting up my gorgeous husband's face. I kissed him and he pulled me in to make love. After lingering in the bed for another hour, both our phones buzzed at the same time.

It was a message from James: Left for Goa early this morning. Driving the BMW. Should arrive by late evening. Will call tomorrow.

PART 8
GOA

Chapter 33

After three weeks of pre-Diwali, Diwali and post-Diwali partying, Aeram and I decided to take a breather and head to Goa. James was at the airport to receive us. He looked fitter, tanner and better in his natural habitat. Aeram sat with him in the front as he drove us to the Albuquerque villa. The orchards reminded me of the times I had walked in them with James, the first time when I had fallen for him, the second time when he took me to his house and the third time with Rachel when she had figured that he was madly in love with me. I had avoided Rachel since we had accidentally met her at Five Spice. She knew James and I loved each other but I did not want to get into situations where I would have to explain ourselves to anyone. Nobody knew James was Aeram's brother and of the bond they shared. I watched the two of them sitting in front of me. From the back, they seemed identical. They were quiet and glanced out of the window once in a while. Occasionally, James would look in the mirror to see me.

"Saysha, say something." I was jolted out of my thoughts by Aeram's voice.

"What?"

He asked, "Don't you think we should clear the jungle on the far corner and plant more trees like these, on the land close to the river?"

I didn't know what to say so I shrugged.

"Just leave it as it is for now," James told Aeram coldly.

I sensed James didn't like anyone doing or saying anything about the trees that he had nurtured so I agreed with him.

Aeram sighed and threw his arms up in the air. "You two drive me nuts!"

James stroked his hair and jibed, "Well, we don't have to try too hard."

Aeram shouted, "Shut up or I'll punch your face."

James grinned, "Only you can tell me shut up and get away with it."

"Yeah, 'nobody messes with James'," Aeram teased him.

James caressed his cheek and in his deep, sexy voice said, "You love that, sweetheart, don't you?" Aeram slapped his hand away.

I giggled. James looked at the mirror and blew me a kiss. I blushed.

"I've missed you, James," Aeram told him as we stopped outside the villa.

James kissed Aeram on his forehead and said, "Come, let's go."

Aeram opened the rear door and carried me out of the car into the villa right up into the bedroom.

I giggled as he lay me onto the bed. He kicked off his shoes, took off his t-shirt and we made love.

When we washed up and went downstairs, James had lunch ready for us on the porch: chicken cafreal, rice, prawn balchao and fried mackerel or *bangda*.

He looked at Aeram and chuckled, "The way you go about it, you'll put rabbits to shame."

Aeram laughed and winked at him. I turned red. Sometimes, they would forget I was standing right there.

James sat next to me. He was deboning the mackerels. Without looking at me he said, "Come with me after lunch."

"Where?"

He raised his eyebrow. "Why do you ask? Don't you trust me?"

I nodded.

James got up and slid the deboned mackerels onto Aeram's plate who looked up with relief and whispered, "Thank you!"

Aeram had a conference call with Monica Cohen's team in the evening so he decided to nap after the heavy lunch. James got the Bullet out and I sat behind him, holding him tight. He had worn the thinnest vest possible and I could feel his heartbeats. We didn't wear our helmets.

He turned his head and kissed me on my cheek.

As we rode along the Mandovi to Old Goa. I began to feel lighter. I moved my hands over his chest and kissed the back of his neck. He threw his head back and gave me a peck. I held him tight. We stopped at the ferry terminal and dismounted. Then he pushed the bike onto the ferry to Divar Island. Once we got on board, he kissed my face and neck. I had missed him. I kissed him lightly on his lips and he let me. We drove around hardly looking at the sights of Malar. He stopped opposite the São Mathias Church and we got off the bike.

I asked, "Why did you just leave like that, James?"

He studied the four-hundred-year-old church's facade. Then, without looking at me, he answered my question. "I couldn't face him after that night with you. Saysha, I have got him back after ages. I don't want to lose him or you. I can't live without you both."

He seemed to be in excruciating pain.

"What's the matter?"

Then he looked at me and said, "We have to draw a line somewhere otherwise we'll mess this whole thing up. These three weeks have given me a lot of time to think. I love both of you and you both love me. We need each other."

I nodded and started to cry.

He put his hand gently on my shoulder. "Saysha," he whispered, "please don't... We cannot lose control of ourselves when we are with each other, Saysha. You are my younger brother's wife."

I scoffed, "I have always been."

James looked into my eyes, caressed my cheek and said, "And in spite of that I love you like crazy. But if we keep doing this and he comes to know, he'll not be able to handle it. He has contemplated suicide before. I don't want us to be the reason for him to think about it again."

I shuddered at the thought. "You're right, James."

"Good girl," he whispered, and kissed me on my forehead.

Chapter 34

We lay in the guest bedroom downstairs on James's bed — all three of us — like in New York, Aeram in the middle, with us on the sides barely getting all our limbs in.

"If I had known you two would join me in bed, I might have bought a bigger one," James joked.

"Hey James, you've got any spooky ghost stories for us?"

"I do, Saysha, but I am not going to take any responsibility for putting this one to sleep." He jokingly pointed to Aeram who rolled his eyes.

"I think you know how to put me to sleep, Saysha," Aeram whispered into my right ear and ran his index finger along my lips.

"You two should get a room," James shouted. I turned red. "We like your bed, James," Aeram chuckled and lay on his back and stared at the ceiling. James slapped his arm. Then he changed the topic. "How was Ibrahim?"

Aeram shrugged and did not answer.

James turned on his side towards Aeram and whispered, "Did he ever hurt you?" His lips were just a couple of inches away from Aeram's cheek.

"No, I guess he was scared of Ammi after the whole Feroz incident. He neither loved me nor hated me. But he loved Sanam."

James stroked his forehead. Aeram sighed. "No one has ever loved me and protected me as much as you have, James, not even Saysha or Ammi. You looked after me when I was born because Marea had died, Ammi was busy working to make ends meet and Papa was too depressed to even take care of himself. He hardly had the energy to get out of bed. You fought off the bullies and you shielded me from Danny when he decided to have a go at me instead of you in this room. And then you looked after me in Mumbai after I lost Ammi and Saysha."

I bit my lip.

A tear rolled down his cheek but before James could wipe it off, Aeram turned and put his head on James's chest. He sniffed, "I wish Ammi had brought you to Delhi with us. I missed you, every day."

"She did what she could do, Aeram, to save us all. Look at us now, we're all together." James stroked his younger brother's hair.

I tried to lighten the mood. "Seriously, James, your idea of a spooky ghost was Ibrahim?"

They both burst out laughing. I heard a thud. James was on the floor, holding his stomach and giggling like a teenaged girl.

Chapter 35

I woke up late in the morning to hear people shouting near the porch. After throwing a netted shrug over my nightdress, I went downstairs to find out what the matter was. I needn't have worried. The men had assembled a soccer team with some of the men who worked in the orchard. All their torsos were bare, some wore shoes and they all wore soccer shorts. Only one player stood out: James. The others just couldn't get the ball from him, not even Aeram. James looked up to see me and in that moment's distraction, Aeram took the ball and scored a goal. He then turned around and blew me a kiss. James smiled and shook his head. They both came towards me while the rest of the men moved towards the orchard to start their work day.

James shouted at me, "If you hadn't come, Saysha, they wouldn't have scored against me." Aeram guffawed. "I am going to take a shower," he said and went upstairs. I thought James might leave to clean up too but he moved closer to me and caressed my lips with his sweaty fingers. He kissed me on my forehead and left.

As we sat down for a brunch of sausages, eggs, salad and *pav*, I finally gathered the courage to tell Aeram, "I want to meet Svetlana again."

They both put their forks down simultaneously. This did not bode well.

Aeram shook his head. "No Saysha. You promised your father and me."

I cried, "Which is why I am asking you, Aeram. I could have sneaked out like last time but I couldn't bear the thought of you being mad at me again."

He caressed my cheek. "I don't like being mad at you, Saysha." Then he looked at James and asked, "What do you think, James?"

I looked at him pleadingly, knowing that Aeram would agree if James thought it was okay.

James smiled and said, "She should meet Svetlana."

Aeram shook his head in disbelief. James put a hand on his shoulder. "Let her figure what is good for her, Aeram. You cannot protect her from everything and everyone. Besides, she is a lot stronger than the two of us put together. You know that."

"She's so naive and kind and pure," Aeram retorted. They were talking about me as if I wasn't there.

"But she is not a fool," James stressed.

Aeram shook his head and looked down. He held his head in his hands. James stood behind him and lightly massaged his shoulders. "Come on, let her go."

Aeram looked at me and scoffed, "You two are driving me insane." He threw his head backwards. His fists were clenched and his nostrils flared. James calmly stroked the furrows on his forehead. Gradually, Aeram calmed down.

James winked at me. "Happy, Saysha?"

I smiled. He blew me a kiss.

This time I didn't book an appointment at Asana spa. James had her number. He had taken it from her, when she had tried to meet me at the restaurant the first time. Aeram had suggested we meet her in a more public place like a restaurant but since it was the peak tourist season, he would have to sit it out or it would be a pathetic afternoon of posing for selfies. James and I chose the popular beach shack, Britto's at Baga, for our meeting with Svetlana.

We had just taken our table when she walked in wearing a tie-and-dye orange kaftan and Prada sunglasses. She greeted us with hugs and kisses. Since she had seen me with James thrice, she had assumed we were a couple. We ordered a fish platter and a couple of beers for us. Svetlana ordered iced lemon water.

"Good to see you, Saysha," she opened the conversation and smiled warmly. "Goa's very busy this time of the year because of the Diwali holidays. Are you enjoying yourself?"

I told her we rarely visited tourist places and just idled around at our villa.

James shifted in his seat. He wanted me to talk to her more but I couldn't think of anything.

Then he suggested, "You should come and visit. It's a plantation on the banks of the Mandovi near the Basilica."

I stared at him.

"I did not know there were plantations there," Svetlana said.

"Ours is the only one. Albuquerque," James told her and sucked on a clam. She was startled when she heard the name.

I realised he was more interested in meeting her than I was.

Lightly placing her hand on mine, Svetlana asked, "Saysha what has kept you busy recently?"

James answered before I could. "You know, we were in New York and we bumped into Igor Lebedinsky. He is Alexandre Lebedinsky's son."

I glared at him but he did not even look at me. He was watching Svetlana, who first turned pink, then deep red. James was enjoying himself. Dimples formed in his cheeks.

Svetlana collected herself and asked me, "Did you read Tatiana's letters?"

It was James's turn to be shocked. I hadn't told him or Aeram about the letters.

I turned red. "I couldn't. They were all in Russian."

"Of course! How stupid of me to not know that," Svetlana said apologetically and glanced at James.

He rolled his eyes and combed his hair with his hand. He did that when he was frustrated. Svetlana watched him. I could sense the tension between the two. This wasn't an ordinary lunch with my aunt.

I tried to lighten the mood by talking about Igor's ambition of becoming an actor but Svetlana wasn't listening to me. She was watching James.

The waiter asked us if we needed anything else. When we said no, James called for the bill.

We rose to leave. The band was playing *That Thing You Do* by The Wonders. Svetlana asked me to hold her bag and invited James to dance with her. No one else was dancing. James and Svetlana jived to the song while I cheered for them. After the song, they both clapped and all the people in the busy restaurant applauded their 'performance'. Svetlana thanked us both for lunch and kissed me goodbye. She only nodded to James.

I sat with James in the front of the car. We drove in silence for a bit till I realized he wasn't taking me home. "Where are we going, James?"

He didn't answer.

"James?"

He took a turn towards the river, found a secluded spot near a paddy field and stopped the car.

I frowned at him. His face gave nothing away.

"What's the matter, James?" I put my hand on his shoulder.

He caressed my cheek and kissed me on my neck. I wanted to kiss him but he thrust his thumb in my mouth so I couldn't do anything while he kissed my face, neck and shoulders. Electricity ran through my body. With my tongue, I finally pushed his thumb out of my mouth but he covered my lips with his fingers. He whispered, "Don't ever kiss me, Saysha. I won't be able to hold myself back. I'll go absolutely crazy. I am already going insane. I want to love you in every possible way but can't so we have to make do with only this much."

Then he stopped. He took both my hands in his and asked, "Saysha, why didn't you tell me about the letters?"

I sighed. "Aeram saw them but he was so mad at me for using Sanam to meet Svetlana last time that I just put them away. All of them were in Russian. I couldn't read any of them."

James threw his hands up and shouted, "Saysha, you think I can't get a Russian in Goa to translate them for you? They're everywhere. Why didn't you ask me?"

My cheeks started feeling hot. I sensed James wanted to know what was in those letters.

He stroked my head. "You have those letters with you here?" I nodded. I hadn't removed them from the Manila in the chest of drawers in our bedroom.

"Let's get them translated into English then." He wasn't asking me.

Chapter 36

"There were only three letters," I told James and handed the Manila envelope to him. He nodded. "I'll bring them back in a day, Saysha," he promised and was off on his Bullet. Aeram watched us from the balcony.

When I went upstairs, I told him about the lunch, the visible tension between Svetlana and James and Tatiana's letters. He just smiled and said nothing. I felt uneasy. He gave me a peck on my cheek and asked me if I wanted to go for a swim at the Taj Hotel's pool. A swim would be great, I thought.

Thankfully, it was late in the evening so we didn't find too many people near the pool and the hotel's staff had cordoned off a portion of it so we had our privacy. That didn't stop people gathering at a distance to take pictures of my gorgeous husband. I started feeling possessive of him and swam close to him. He took me in his arms and kissed me on my cheeks. A couple of paparazzi managed to get our pictures.

On our way back to the villa, Aeram stopped the car in the woods between the river and the orchard. His hand grazed my thigh. Soon, we were making love in the car. The last time we had done that was in Shimla, a long time ago. Before we started for home, Aeram pointed to the trees. "I want to clear this and build a promenade but James is adamant that this wilderness should remain as it is."

I was curious. "And you can't change James's plans?"

He firmly said, "No."

"You're scared of him, Aeram," I teased him.

He got very serious, pressed my hand, and said, "Yes."

I frowned. How could my super-rich and powerful husband be scared of an older brother he had united with only a few years ago, who had been poor until a couple of months ago and who still worked as our driver and my husband's stunt-double?

He chuckled to himself and started the car.

When we reached home, James was waiting for us on the porch. One look at us and he knew what we had been up to. He shook his head. Aeram threw his wet swimming trunks at him and it dropped right at James's feet. He laughed out loud as I made my way up the stairs to our bedroom.

At dinner, Aeram broke the news. "Guys, I have to go to Bangalore tomorrow and will be there for three days."

"Why?" James asked him without looking up. He ladled the sorpotel onto a heap of rice on his plate.

Aeram sighed. "Zarine told me I had committed to these guys six months ago. I don't remember but since they've paid me the full money, I have to show up."

"What exactly have you signed up for, Aeram?" I was irritated. My workaholic husband did not know how to relax.

He shrugged and said, "There's a speaking gig at IIM in Bangalore. It's a youth event or something. Then there's also a jewellery store opening there. Apparently, they want me to open the Mysore store too. And then there are some interviews lined up."

James scoffed, "And you've just found out, haven't you?"

Aeram nodded. He was embarrassed.

James rolled his eyes and shouted, "Saysha, this guy is not a control-freak. He doesn't even control his schedules."

He had a point. Aeram was controlled by everyone else, his producers, Zarine, his tech team and James. I felt bad for him. He smiled meekly and apologised, "I'm sorry, Saysha, just three days."

James demanded, "What time do you have to leave?"

"Seven at the airport. Zarine will meet me there and then we'll go together." Then, as an afterthought, he looked at me, "Do you want to come?"

Before I could answer, James said, "No, leave her here. I want her for myself."

Aeram turned red and his lips quivered. He was still very insecure about James and me.

James laughed and came round the table. He put his arms around Aeram's neck, bent down and gave him a tight hug and a kiss on his cheek. "My dear little brother, I am just pulling your leg. If you weren't hopping all over the place both of us would have joined you. But you have to entice me with something more than a jewellery store opening. Throw in some bikes, for example. Why don't you sign up for that kind of stuff?"

Aeram relaxed and laughed, "They don't pay as much as the guys who trade gold."

James lifted his brother's chin. "It's always about money, Aeram, isn't it?"

Aeram shrugged. "It is, and I don't understand why you don't get it."

James tousled Aeram's hair. "The things that feed your soul make you happy, darling. Not just money or possessions."

"But you need money to get that stuff." Aeram stressed on the word, 'need'.

"You've had more than enough money and still been miserable. You're brilliant as an actor and even more as a businessman but even all that money couldn't have saved this villa for us. And this is the only place I've seen you happy."

Aeram looked down. James said, "I didn't care much if we got the estate or not. I have lived without it most of my life and the title doesn't define me as a person. Only James can define James. But this is the only place you've felt safe and at home. It means a lot more to me and so it became my fight. And James has never lost a fight."

I smiled.

"Thank you for that, James, but I have to go to Bangalore tomorrow and you will drive me to the airport," Aeram said.

"Yes, sir," James saluted him.

Aeram laughed and hugged him tight. "What would I do without you, James?"

"You would be a miserable rich bastard. By the way, Saysha, it was my idea, the shoot in Shimla."

What? I was surprised.

Aeram told James, "Shh...I still haven't told her."

"Told me what, Aeram?" I was furious.

James laughed, "You think it takes a week to shoot a bloody commercial?"

Aeram picked up his glass and threw water on him. James's white vest was soaking wet. "Oh, you're so dead," he shouted and picked up a jug of water and poured it on Aeram's head. "Damn! James," he shouted and picked up another glass of water to throw.

I had to stop them before they turned the whole place upside down.

"Stop it, you two," I shouted.

They stood like two punished schoolboys.

I ordered them. "Sit and eat, first. We were having dinner, for God's sake!"

They sat and then Aeram started laughing. "Saysha, you could have been the leader of a regiment."

James guffawed. I shouted at him, "What are you laughing for? And what the hell were you saying about the shoot in Shimla?"

Aeram said softly, "I knew you were in Shimla, Saysha, at St Lawrence. James had managed to track you down with his connections when I had told him how miserable I was without you. When the director of the commercial suggested Mussoorie, I asked him to shoot in Shimla. I had planned to stay for a week to look for you but then you came to the shoot. James was in the van with me and we were actually planning our next move to find you when the assistant brought me your note."

Unbelievable!

"I love you, Saysha, and I missed you so much." Haltingly, he confessed, "I got drunk one day and talked with James about the different ways of committing suicide." I choked. James balled his fist and was biting his thumb. Aeram glanced at him and then turned towards me. "James suggested that we should look for you instead of just giving up on life. We started by stalking all your old Facebook contacts I had known before you had closed your account and found that Rachel had been with you in Delhi and Shimla. James knew someone at St Lawrence and we managed to trace you."

I stared at James who was tucking into his sorpotel-rice. There was something about him that didn't sit right. He saw me watching him and smiled. He knew that I knew that he wasn't the man we thought he was. He was too much of a genius to be just a stunt-double and driver. He spoke English well, was extremely well-read and very talented for a man of limited means. He was at ease wherever he travelled, even in New York or Alhandra, much more than someone like me who had grown up in posh south Delhi. He had a vast network of people who would get things done or find information for him, though we had no idea who his friends were. It was up to me to get something out of him over the next three days without Aeram around to distract me.

That night, for the first time in over a year of knowing him, I googled James Christian Albuquerque. The pages were full of news of him taking on Archbishop Patrick. He had never given any interviews in spite of being inundated by journalists' calls. He had only issued statements through his lawyer, Manohar Salgaonkar. He never discussed anything about it with anyone.

There were pages dedicated to him and Aeram and how good they both looked. I scrolled and scrolled, there was nothing more that I could learn. He had never opened any social media accounts so there was nothing other than what the press had. He still preferred SMS instead of WhatsApp and through this whole year, I had never seen him send out an email.

Then it struck me. In spite of being so openly gay, I had never seen James with a man, a partner. I had seen him with Joe a few times but they never even held hands in public. The only man he hugged, held, caressed and kissed was his brother. I was almost on the verge of giving up and turning in, when on the twentieth page there was a two-liner in a language I didn't know. I put the text in Google Translate, to figure what the original language was. It was Portuguese.

Google Translate suggested in English:

"The investigation was carried out by James Christian Albuquerque in Alhandra. The warehouse belonged to one of the largest mining companies in Europe."

It was dated to five years ago, a little before Aeram had moved to Mumbai to find him. Or did James find Aeram?

"What are you looking at?" Aeram started to get up. I didn't want to talk to him so I kissed him and he fell off to sleep.

Chapter 37

By the time I woke up the next day, Aeram had already boarded the flight to Bangalore. James was nowhere to be seen so I decided to give myself a nice long bath. I heard the sound of the car. James was back. I took my time to get dressed in dark blue jeans and white t-shirt. If I had to get him to talk, my behaviour around him would have to be normal. Only, I didn't feel normal. The whole year seemed like a lie.

James had laid out a breakfast of bread, eggs, sausages and fruits at the dining table. He sat there drumming his fingers on the table while light streamed in through the blinds and lit up his stunning features.

I took the chair opposite him. He smiled. I didn't. He raised his eyebrows. A tear rolled down my cheek. Then another. He got up from his chair and sat next to me. "Saysha," he whispered, "please don't…" A dam burst and I hugged him and sobbed.

"What's the matter, darling?"

He gently kissed me on my cheeks.

I took out my phone and showed him the two-liner in Portuguese. His jaw tightened very slightly. Then he chuckled, "This made you cry? Why?"

"Because you lied to me, to us," I shouted between sobs.

The smile vanished from his face. He brought his forehead to mine. His lips were just an inch away from my lips. I could feel his breath on me and wanted to kiss him. He whispered, "It's not deception. It's protection."

He kissed me on my forehead, rose from his seat and pulled the chair opposite me. Buttering his toast, he ordered, "Pack your bags for three days, Saysha. We're going. We'll be back on the day Aeram returns to Goa."

I asked, "Where are we going?"

"To see the other river, Zuari," is all he said and took a bite. I kicked my chair to stand up and watched him. He sliced the pork sausage without looking at me. I cried loudly and ran up the staircase.

"You played me, James. I love you and you played me," I shouted at him as he opened the car's rear door.

"I love you more than anything in the world, Saysha. I always have and will forever," he said very seriously and shut the door.

"Then you have to tell me everything from the beginning."

He fastened his seat-belt and shook his head. "I can't, Saysha. I cannot compromise your safety."

A tear rolled down my cheek.

"Saysha," he whispered, "Please don't... okay, let's do this... You can ask me ten questions. Nothing more. I will choose to explain the answer only if I think it will not endanger you. Okay?"

I sniffed and nodded.

"Ask wisely," he said and started the car.

I began with the obvious question:

"Are you gay?"

He sighed before answering, "No."

He must have noticed the shocked expression on my face in the mirror. "I was thrown out of the school in Mapusa because I finally found the courage to beat one of my abusers. Since an investigation would have resulted in a closet full of skeletons tumbling out, they labelled me gay and made me infamous. Initially, I believed them and tried to have a boyfriend, the

Turkish student who taught me how to make coffee. But two sessions with him and we both realized that we would be better as flatmates than anything else. The gay identity helped with my job, though."

I bit my lip. "Does Aeram know?"

James shrugged, "I think he suspects because I have never brought a man home but he respects me too much to ask the question."

"Where do you work, James?"

He answered while looking out of the window, "Interpol."

"Why were you so interested in my meeting with Svetlana?"

He shook his head. "I can't answer that question, right now."

"Did you find Aeram or did he find you?"

"I made myself available when I knew he would be coming for me."

"You knew about the wills before you met Aeram, right?"

He whistled. "You're so smart, Saysha, which is why I love you so much."

I blushed. He saw me in the mirror, blew me a kiss and continued, "Richard bequeathed the estates to me before he died. He knew he had cancer so he had everything planned with Manohar *mama* as my guardian and Farah as the custodian of his wills. Danny and Father Patrick wanted to get rid of me for the same reason. Aeram and Sanam wouldn't have been able to inherit the estates because they were Farah and Richard's children, officially, and never baptized."

"How did you end up in Alhandra five years ago?"

He chuckled, "Since you've figured that I am smarter than most stunt-doubles and drivers, I'll tell you. Both Aeram and I are blessed with Marea's intelligence. Sanam got her looks from her but the rest is all Richard's. Farah always knew about my whereabouts. Manohar *mama* and she kept in touch all the time. When I was thrown out of the school in Mapusa, she was intimated. She pleaded with Ibrahim to let me join them in Delhi but he refused. I stayed with Manohar *mama* and finished my schooling in Panjim. Manohar *mama* is very well-connected so schools didn't have a problem taking his ward in. Since his practice was in Panjim, he would drop me at school, go to work, then pick me up. I would hang around in his office for a few hours and then we would go home to Mapusa. On some weekends, he would drive me down to the villa where I would go to Mamma's house. When I turned eighteen, I learned that

Papa had made provision for me to study in Lisbon in Portugal. I graduated from Universidade de Lisboa and was offered a scholarship to study International Relations at Geneva in Switzerland. I did a summer in New York, another in London. One thing led to another and I ended up at Interpol in Lyon in France."

I was going to ask him my next question when he volunteered a little more information. "I know eight languages, Saysha: English, Konkani, Portuguese, Hindi, German, French, Spanish and Russian."

My eyes popped out when he mentioned Russian. I remembered Tatiana's letters. He seemed to know what was on my mind. He smiled and told me, "You'll get them in Mumbai. Ask me your next question."

"With that kind of education and such good looks why did you have to work as Aeram's stunt-double and driver?"

He laughed. "To protect him. I can't tell you anything else about it."

I scoffed, "So bringing me back into his life was part of your plan to protect him?"

He winced. "Yes, I wanted to save him from misery so we made the plan. But I had never imagined that I would fall in love with you, Saysha. There was no plan there. It just happened."

I bit my lip to prevent myself from crying.

"Do you really love Aeram or are you just using him for your mission?"

He glared at me. "I don't know what kind of monster you think I am but I'll do anything in the world to protect him and you, even if it costs me my life."

Then he said, "Your ten questions are over, Ma'am, and we have arrived at our destination."

Chapter 38

We drove past a beautiful church. James looked out of the window and said, "That's St Andrew's. Welcome to Goa Velha."

What? We had just left Velha Goa or Old Goa and now we were in Goa Velha which looked like an old city but wasn't the same. I was so confused.

James started laughing. "This is on the Zuari in Ilhas. It was founded by Afonso de Albuquerque at the site of the ancient port city, Gopakapatana."

He took me to a relatively modest-looking hotel. "This is the best they have here. Besides, we'll not be staying in our rooms the whole day so for a few hours at night, this should suffice," he told me.

He led me to my room. His was across the corridor. The room was adequate but comfortable. James lingered at the door. Then he closed it behind him and came charging towards me. He wrapped his arms around me and kissed me on my lips, a long, deep kiss. I kissed him back. One thing led to another and we were soon making out in my bed. I started unbuttoning his shirt. He hadn't worn the Cross. I felt his hands go up my t-shirt and caress my left breast. Then suddenly, he stopped and started to get up. I tried to pull him into the bed but he was buttoning up his shirt. Then he knelt in front of me and took both my hands in his. A tear rolled down his cheek. He looked into my eyes and said, "Don't ever say that to me again, Saysha, that I played you. I love you too much, too deeply. Had it been anyone but him, I would have fought for you. I would have made you mine. Aeram doesn't stand a chance in a fight against me. He knows that. But I love him too much so I can't think of hurting him." He caressed my lips with his thumb and left.

It took me all of fifteen minutes to process what he had just said. I picked up my bag and walked to the door opposite my room and knocked on it. He opened it. James was wearing only his black Adidas soccer shorts. He saw my bag and raised an eyebrow.

"Since we're hardly going to stay in our rooms in such a modest hotel, there's no reason why we should bother spending on an extra room," I told him and pushed the door open, plonking my bag on his foot. I then stretched myself out on his bed. He shook his head, and shouted, "Saysha, you're driving me insane."

That was the first time we made love.

My head rested on his warm smooth chest. I listened to his beating heart. Then my phone buzzed. It was a message from Aeram: Where are the two of you?

"What do we tell him, James?"

"I'll tell him," James replied and texted Aeram: We're at Goa Velha, Ilhas. Will go back when you're back from Bangalore.

There was a long silence on Aeram's part. Then he just replied with an OK.

James sighed and stroked my hair. "Can I ask you something, Saysha?"

"Yes," I whispered and kissed his chest.

"Why did you marry him?"

I lifted my head. He sat upright and looked at me. I was fidgety. He stroked my arm and said, "You knew he wasn't a normal guy. He never had friends, forget about girlfriends. And then suddenly he became very famous but very miserable as well. Why did someone like you want to marry him?"

I bit my lip. This is something that I had asked myself several times over. I hesitated. He pressed me close to him and kissed my hair. I replied, "I didn't."

He frowned and turned my face towards him. "What?"

A tear trickled down my cheek. "I told him no every time he asked me because he was so possessive of me. But at the prom, when he suddenly revealed himself, we couldn't hide our relationship anymore and so the only way together I thought was…"

"Marriage?" He completed my sentence. He threw his hands in the air and shouted, "Saysha, you've given your life to a man who has serious mental health issues that he doesn't even want to acknowledge. He loves you like crazy, yes, but spending your life on a rollercoaster was quite an idea of a future."

I caressed his cheek. "James, I did not know there was any other way to love or be loved till you walked with me in the orchard." He kissed me again.

Then he whispered, "The problem with Aeram is that he lost everything too soon in life and then he got everything really quickly. Somewhere in between, he didn't mature emotionally. The man doesn't realise what a gift you are to him so he uses you just for sex."

I scolded him, "James, I love him. He can use me for whatever he wants."

He kissed me on my forehead. "Saysha, you deserve to be loved, not used. Aeram's a very nice guy. I love him dearly. If you guys had waited five years or even three, you might have created something more special."

"What do we do now, James? I can't just leave him," I cried.

He exhaled loudly. "We'll figure something."

Chapter 39

We were sitting in a small fisherman's motorboat heading upstream Zuari. James held me tight. His brown hair glistened in the early morning sun. He looked like a Hollywood star in his jeans, khaki shirt and Prada sunglasses. I thought of the previous night. We had made love a few times.

Somewhere, in the middle of wilderness between mangroves and reeds, James spoke in Konkani. The fisherman stopped the boat. We started our hike from there, stopping for breath and water and eating the breakfast of tomato and cheese sandwiches the hotel had packed for us. We passed through a couple of tiny villages with colourful houses, where in some cases, each wall was painted a different colour. Under the Portuguese rule, Goan houses were not allowed to be painted white. Only churches were white. After an hour and a half of trudging up and down the slopes and staining our jeans and sneakers with red soil, we finally arrived at our destination: a huge open-cast mine. The earth had been brutally disembowelled by a hydraulic excavator. Trucks carried the red earth out to processing plants on the banks of the river where they would extract iron ore. Large swathes of the forest had been cleared and where a hill had once stood, was now a cavity. It was horrific!

"This is just one of them," said James. He pointed his finger away from the direction we had walked and told me, "You keep going, you'll find them lined one after another. Same thing over there."

As we slowly walked back towards the river, my heart felt heavy. I loved Goa and its natural beauty. What James had shown me that morning was brutal. On our way back in the boat, I put my head on his shoulder and wept silently. He did not wipe my tears.

"The mines are killing this river, Saysha. All those minerals are poisons — they're all coming in here." James spoke passionately.

Four months ago, Aeram's movie, *Gone Goa Gone* had released. It was about mining in Goa and the damage it had caused to the communities here. But no screen, no matter how large it was, could have shown us what we had seen with our own eyes that day.

There was a reason why James had taken me there but he did not tell me.

When we reached Goa Velha, James asked me, "Lunch?" I nodded. We ate a simple lunch of rice and fish curry at a small dining hall near St Andrew's Church.

We then went back to our hotel room. The trudge through the forest had made us both muddy and sweaty. James headed straight to the shower while I looked through the contents of my bag to find something to wear. Suddenly, I found his wet arms around me and he picked me up. He had only his towel wrapped around his waist. He took me straight into the shower with my clothes still on. He pulled out my t-shirt and peeled off my jeans and undergarments as if we showered together every day. There was no awkwardness between us, unlike the first time Aeram and I had sat in the bath together in Shimla. The red earth from my jeans collected on the bathroom floor. James ran the water to clean it off. He soaped his hands and ran them over my body. Then he dropped his towel and in a deep sexy voice said, "I like to play dirty."

We lay in each other's arms after a long session in the shower. Our lips were almost touching. A thought crossed my mind and I frowned.

James caressed my back and asked softly. "What are you thinking about?"

"You've slept with over a hundred people, James. What's my number?"

He tugged at my hair so hard that I winced.

"James, you're hurting me," I screamed.

"And so are you by asking me that question." He looked menacing. I was scared. He let go of my hair and kissed my face. "Don't ever humiliate my love for you like that, Saysha."

I bit my lip.

He caressed my cheek with his thumb. "I have had women before, but I have never been in love, Saysha. It's been you since the day I saw you."

"But not a hundred, right?"

He laughed and caressed my cheek, "No, maybe three or four."

Chapter 40

We had to pick up Aeram from the airport in Panjim on our way back to Albuquerque. This was our last day in Goa. The next day we would be leaving for Mumbai.

Aeram greeted us with a wide smile and big hugs. I jumped into the backseat while he sat with James in the front.

He asked James, "Why did you guys suddenly go to Ilhas?"

"I wanted to show her the mines," he told him calmly.

Aeram turned around and asked me, "It's gut-wrenching to watch that, right?"

I nodded without looking at him.

"I missed you both," Aeram said. James stroked his hair and told him, "Next time, inaugurate a bike or luxury car showroom, not some stupid jewellery store."

The arrogant ass of my husband retorted, "Well, the jewellery showroom ensures that you drive a BMW and not a Ford Fiesta."

"Always about money, darling. Work less and live more and you'll find happiness," James told him.

"I work hard so that you two can live off me. Actually, three, Sanam included. Her credit card bills ensure I keep cutting ribbons everywhere."

James chuckled. "Do something for yourself, Aeram, for a change. What makes you happy, like really happy? Something that money cannot buy. Something you can't live without."

Aeram thought for a while. James glanced at him a couple of times. Then Aeram spoke as if he was talking to himself, "Lying on your bed in Marea's room, watching the ceiling and you stroking my head. Or whenever we play soccer. Also, that time when the two of us balanced that big crate of beer and the packets of food on the Bullet and drove it back from Panjim. That was crazy." James laughed.

Something tugged at my heart. I realized Aeram's happiness was only in the company of James. Nobody else. Not even me. He had not mentioned that I made him happy. I felt less guilty about sleeping with James who was watching me in the mirror. I blew him a kiss. He smiled.

"Give up that high-flying lifestyle of yours and stay here," James told Aeram as we entered the gates of the orchard. "You can look after all of this."

"And what will you do, Sherlock?" It was the first time Aeram had given a hint about his brother's real profession. In Goa, in James's company, he had finally let his guard down.

James laughed, "You play me in your movies. I save your gorgeous ass in the real world."

I smiled. He looked at me in the mirror and blew me a kiss.

Aeram sighed. "I've missed you, James."

He had spoken to me only once during the whole journey. I bit my lip.

When I got out of the car in front of the villa, Aeram scooped me up with his arms and took me to our bedroom.

Late at night, the three of us stood in the balcony looking at the full moon. Aeram closed his eyes and tilted his head upwards. "You know, I talk to the moon sometimes," he told us, without really speaking to us. James moved close to him. Their arms were almost touching. "The moon is my protector, James," Aeram said, opening his eyes. "It protects me from myself. It is always with me, for me." It didn't make any sense to me. Sometimes, what Aeram said was too deep. I glanced at James who looked like he had swallowed a bitter pill. He wrapped his arms around Aeram and whispered into his ear,

"Darling, I will always be there to protect you. I promise." A tear trickled down Aeram's cheek.

PART 9

MUMBAI

Chapter 41

Rachel's text interrupted my daydream about James. "Hi! You're back! Let's meet at my house."

"Sure," I replied.

Aeram walked in and gave me a peck on my cheek.

I asked him, "Hey Rachel wants to meet at her place. Do you want to join us?"

Aeram shook his head. "I'd love to, Saysha, but Zarine's got a podcast lined up for me in an hour."

I envied Zarine. She had the greater share of my husband's time. She was Imran's sister and they had known each other since they were kids, they were more friends than colleagues. In fact, Aeram never really counted her among his friends, but I knew that she was his closest friend after James.

"Ok then, I'll go alone," I got up from my chair.

"Take James," Aeram suggested.

I didn't want to take James to Rachel's house, especially after she had figured that we were in love with each other. It would be embarrassing.

James walked in that very moment.

"There you are," Aeram turned around and shouted, "Please take Saysha to Rachel's house, James. I have to do a podcast."

James smiled and nodded.

I wore a grey summer dress and white kitten heels. James checked me out as I walked out of the building to sit next to him in the car. He put his hand on my thigh and felt me up under the dress. It gave me goosebumps. I tried to brush his hand off but he kept doing it, all the while keeping his eyes on the road in the front. When we reached Rachel's apartment building, I found her standing in the balcony. She screamed, "Bring James as well." I looked at him. "I'll park and join you. Go ahead," he said.

"Where's he?" Rachel enquired as soon as she opened the door.

I blushed. "He's parking. He'll join us."

"Hi Saysha," said another voice. I wasn't expecting company.

"Hello John Uncle," I replied and hugged him.

"Dad's visiting me for a couple of days. He has a seminar here. This is the first time he is staying in my apartment," Rachel proudly announced.

"That's great, Uncle."

"You guys came back from Goa this week?"

"Yes, Uncle."

Someone rang the doorbell. Rachel opened it. James smiled at her. "Hi Rachel."

"Finally, James! My house is better than a car-park," she chirped. James laughed. Then she turned to John Uncle. "Dad, this is James Albuquerque, Aeram's stuntman-cum-friend. James, this is my dad, Lt General John Countinho."

A weird expression appeared on John Uncle's face for a few seconds and then he smiled at James and shook his hand firmly, "Nice to meet you."

"Dad, James took down the high and mighty Archbishop Patrick," Rachel excitedly told her father.

I could see James was embarrassed. Thankfully, Uncle came to his rescue. He turned to James and asked, "Young man, would you want to accompany me for a walk and let the ladies do the talking?"

Rachel wanted to keep James with us, but he took up Uncle's offer.

When they both left, I scolded her, "Rachel, you didn't tell me your dad was here." I wouldn't have brought James along if I had known Uncle was visiting.

She laughed. "It was a surprise, darling. Where's Aeram?"

I shrugged. "He has a podcast."

"He's such a workaholic. No wonder, I always see you with James."

I blushed.

"I like him," Rachel said.

I raised my eyebrows.

She combed her long permed hair with her fingers and said, "I wish you had met this one before you met that nutcase."

I laughed. Rachel had always made fun of Aeram's eccentricities.

She brought out the brownies, Old Monk and Coke, much to my delight. I loved her cakes.

"Bless you, Rachel!"

She put the tray down and tied her hair up with a rubber-band into a bun. "Why is he only a stuntman, *yaar*? I wish he was a little more ambitious."

I smiled.

"Is he not gay or is he gay but he likes you?" She asked, passing me a plate with a brownie. Then she poured 30 ml of rum into a tall glass, dropped two cubes of ice and topped it with Coke.

I laughed. "Why don't you just ask him Rachel?"

James and John Uncle entered the apartment.

"What are you laughing about?" John Uncle demanded.

Rachel answered, "Nothing really, Dad. Just some old stuff from school."

"Well, I'll leave you three alone. Give the young man something nice to drink." He frowned at the bottle of Old Monk.

"Old Monk's fine, Sir," James said.

As soon as Rachel's father left the room, she started flirting with James. But I didn't feel possessive about him. He was very sure of himself.

"James, you're the hottest gay guy around." Rachel ogled at his chest. He had left the top three buttons of his shirt open.

He smiled.

Pointing towards me, she quipped, "So she has made you swing the other way, has she not?"

I turned a deep red. James seemed to be enjoying the conversation.

"I told you, Rachel, I always keep my options open." He suggestively ran his tongue along his lower lip.

Rachel's heart skipped a beat.

"That husband of hers might kill you." She was playing with him.

James looked at me and grinned, "Well, she's worth dying for."

I squirmed. This was getting very embarrassing. "Okay, Rachel, I guess we should leave."

I got up but James remained seated. His jaw had tightened.

Then he asked her, "How's Cyrus, Rachel?"

She clicked her tongue. "Well, we haven't spoken for a bit. I guess he's busy."

He frowned and asked, "Are you sure?"

I wondered what James was up to.

"Well, from what I heard, he was busy playing tongue hockey with Tripti at Disha's birthday bash yesterday. Weren't you invited?"

My jaw dropped in shock. Rachel was horrified. She stood up and screamed, "You're joking, right?"

James shook his head.

She looked at me. I didn't know what to say. She dialled Cyrus and gave him the firing of his life pacing up and down the tiny balcony. James and I quietly left through the front door.

As I strapped my seatbelt I asked him, "Cyrus and Tripti?"

He wore his Prada sunglasses and started the car. I couldn't read his expression.

"But why did you tell Rachel? She could have found out on her own. It wasn't your business," I scolded James.

He ran his thumb on my lip. "She teased you and I couldn't tolerate it."

I kissed his hand.

He smiled, "You'll have to do better than that, Saysha."

I giggled.

Then I remembered John Uncle's expression when he first saw James. I asked him, "Why did Uncle look at you that way?"

He stopped caressing my thigh and threw his head back. "God, Saysha! You notice everything."

I waited for his answer.

"Well, he knows me. I conducted some lectures at ARTRAC, the Army Training Centre, when he was there. He didn't know how to react when Rachel introduced me as a stuntman."

"You were in Shimla?"

"Duh, yes! When the two of you were rolling in the grass outside the cottage in Mashobra."

I cringed. "You saw that?"

"No, but your husband can be quite graphic when he is describing stuff to his elder brother."

I buried my face in my hands.

James laughed.

"Was it John Uncle who told you that I was at St Lawrence in Shimla?"

"Yes. We had met a few times in Delhi and during one of the conversations, I dropped your father's name. He then told me how you were sent away as punishment."

A few painful memories came back. I looked down. James leaned over and kissed my cheek.

Then he asked, "Why were you punished?"

"I had just broken up with Aeram and was in a bad mood and had yelled at my mother and brother." I looked away so he couldn't see me crying.

James touched my shoulder. "Do you want to talk about it, Saysha?"

We were sitting in a traffic jam at Kemps Corner. There was plenty of time for us to talk and so I told him everything, about how Aeram insisted that I agree to marry him, how he had said that he would not allow me to marry anyone else and then I would be forced to marry him, about how we were scared of losing each other again so we decided to get married.

That James was shocked was an understatement. He took off his sunglasses and shouted. "What? Are you both insane? He is, but you? Damn! Saysha. Did you even love each other or were you just enjoying the thrill of sneaking out and making out like teenagers usually do?"

He had hit the nail on its head. The more I thought about it, the more I realized that we should have waited to get married, known each other better. We had only been together for less than three months over a period of three and a half years when we had decided to marry. We didn't have a plan. We did not know what our life together would look like. Aeram was a workaholic and his celebrity status meant I could not socialize with just about anyone I wanted to. He didn't have time for me and I had all the time to feel lonely. Our relationship had distanced me from my family and friends since we were in college. The only person who gave me company and cared for me was James and I had fallen in love with him barely three months after Aeram and I had married.

James caressed my cheek. I turned towards him and kissed him on his lips. He kissed me back. I noticed the women passengers in the back of the black-and-yellow taxi next to us were watching us. I didn't care. I kissed James again and again, unbuttoning a couple more buttons of his shirt and running my hand all the way down his chest. He moaned.

"If you asked me now and I wasn't married already, I would marry you tomorrow," I announced, when we broke away. The traffic started to crawl.

He shook his head. "No, Saysha. If I ask you to marry me right now, you will say, you want to live with me first. You will want to see the kind of lifestyle I can offer you, see if your friends and family fit into it, see how often I have to travel and whether you can accompany me or not and then think about marrying me. Do you understand?"

I nodded and kissed him.

The traffic finally started to move. I tucked a strand of hair behind my ear. "What will we do, James? I cannot live without you but I cannot hurt him in any way."

James pressed my hand and told me, "We'll figure a way out. Leave it to me. I am the only one who can tell him and make him understand. But I have to finish other stuff first."

Chapter 42

I was creating a spreadsheet for the props we needed for *Darbaar* when James walked in. He had a Manila envelope in his hand — Tatiana's letters. He watched me open the envelope. The smaller ones inside were sealed and identical to the original ones. He read my mind before I could ask. "They're yours, Saysha. Only you can open and read them. I just wanted to do something for you that would help you understand your mother. I don't want to know what's in there, unless you want me to know." I smiled. He kissed me on my forehead and left me with my letters.

Each of the smaller envelopes had two sheets of paper, the original letter in Russian and the printed translation in English.

I opened the first letter and read it:

Dear Svetlana,

I have arrived in New Delhi. It's a nice house where I am staying. Indian families give you a lot of food to eat. I might become fat in a month. I miss you, Alex and Mother. Come and visit India sometime. I will start college next week.

Love,

Tati

It looked more like a note than a letter.

I opened the second one. It was written three months after the first one.

Dear Svet,

I am in love. The family I am staying with, their son Karanjit came home from army training in Dehradun. It's a hill station in the Himalayas. He's very handsome and he took me to see all the beautiful places in Delhi. He told me he will take me to see the Taj Mahal in Agra as well. College is okay. I made a few friends here. English is a problem I have. Everyone talks English, Hindi or Punjabi. There is only one other Russian in my class, Oleg Oblonsky. He doesn't talk to anyone and keeps studying all the time. I have two Indian friends in class, Pramila and Mansi. Mansi took me to her house to meet her family. They were very nice and even gifted me a salwar kameez. It's a pretty Indian dress in dark pink. I am going to wear it for Diwali. It's a big festival in India. They decorate everything with lights. I wish you could come and see. I want you to meet Karanjit. Maybe we can talk over the phone. Give my love to Mother and Alex.

Love,

Tati

Finally, I opened the third one. It was written four months after the previous one.

Dear Svet,

Why haven't you written to me? Have you not got my letters? Ask Mother or Alex to write as well. I miss you all. I have news for you. I am pregnant, twelve weeks. I am very stressed. Karanjit too. His mother wants me to abort the baby. I don't know what to do. The only other Russian I know is Oleg but I can't ask him for help. Can you come here? I need your help or Alex's. Call me please. You don't even answer my calls. I don't have money to call every day. Please answer this letter.

Love,

Tati

She was very upset. A tear rolled down my cheek. At that moment, James walked in with Aeram's costumes. He dumped them on the sofa and sat next to me. "Saysha, please don't…" he whispered and put his hand on my shoulder. I buried my head in his chest and started crying.

He asked, "Do you want me to read them?"

"Yes," I said between sobs.

He pulled out the Russian originals first. Then he glanced at the translation. He was concentrating hard on something. His forehead had furrowed.

Curious, I asked him, "What's the matter, James? Is the translation, okay?"

He kissed my forehead. "It's perfect, darling," but I could tell there was something in the letters that was quite alarming.

He gently folded the translations and gave them to me. He folded the Russian originals and put them in the pocket of his shirt. He got up and told me, "Aeram's going to be coming here in five minutes for his costume trials. I'll see you guys in a bit."

Aeram walked in and saw me with the translated letters. He wanted to read them too. I gave them to him. He smiled and kissed me. "I love you, Saysha," he said. "I love you too, Aeram," I told him. Then he gave me a weird look.

I shrugged and asked, "What?"

He rubbed his forehead to erase the creases that had formed. "I know you love each other, Saysha. You're madly in love with him and he is crazy about you. I am not going to ask either of you what you were doing in Ilhas."

I bit my lip out of guilt.

Then he looked into my eyes and told me, "But I can't live without you and so I will never let you go." He put both his arms around me and pressed my body to his. He held me so tight that I couldn't breathe. I tried to loosen his hold but he didn't budge. "Aeram, you're hurting me," my stifled voice cried out. A wicked smile played on his lips. "You cannot leave me, Saysha, ever," he whispered and bit my earlobe. It hurt. He watched me flinch but didn't say anything. He just kept staring at me with a strange expression in his eyes. It was as if he was fighting something within himself.

After what seemed like a long time, he gave me a kiss on my cheek and released me. I gasped for air and he left the room to go downstairs to the study. I broke down. That was the first and the only time Aeram had done something to hurt me. I cried not because it hurt. I cried because he had enjoyed hurting me. When James walked in an hour later, he sensed something was wrong. I didn't tell him anything.

Chapter 43

Zarine had invited us for dinner at her house in Tardeo, just the three of us along with Imran and Sanghamitra. Imran had proposed to Sangha after dating her for four years and they were due to marry late next year. Zarine wanted to celebrate.

While I was jealous of the attention and time Zarine got from my husband, I greatly admired her. Eight years older than Aeram and Imran, she managed to keep them both in check. She was a workaholic and had decided that she would never marry. As we raised our toasts to Imran and Sangha at the dinner table, I remembered how we had missed all of this in our rush to marry. There had been no announcements, no friends, no toasts, no parties, just a whiplash from the media for being so secretive about the most important function of our lives.

I sat between the two men I loved more than anything else in the world. One had given me an extraordinary life, the other, a true sense of self-worth. I had remained in the shadow of one till the other had shown me that I could cast my own shadow. One thought it was his duty to protect me, the other empowered me to protect myself. I had loved Aeram with every bit of my heart until the moment he told me that he would never let me go because he couldn't live without me. He hadn't asked me what I wanted. That was the moment, I had decided to leave him.

A tap on my shoulder brought me back to the candlelit dinner we were at. James smiled at me and pointed to the cake I had not yet touched. He had figured there was something going on in my head.

Aeram sat with James in the front on our drive back home. I watched Haji Ali pass by. The moon shone on the dome. I prayed silently for things to be put right, hoping no hearts would be broken in the process. I had loved Aeram too deeply. I couldn't bear the thought of making him miserable.

James suddenly parked the car in a rare empty spot on the sea face near the juice centre. "Come, let's take a walk," he told us. Aeram looked around at the people who were there for their late-night strolls and juices. He shook his head. James opened the rear door for me and told him, "I am taking Saysha with me, Aeram. You know she'll like a walk. If you want to join us, please do."

I got out of the car and started walking with James. We had walked a few paces when we heard the car door slam shut. Aeram was walking towards us. He had worn his sunglasses and cap, which was stupid because it attracted more attention.

James laughed and shouted, "Take them off, man!"

Aeram hesitated, then took them off and handed them to a child beggar who was delighted to get a gift from a superstar. He wore them and danced all around till he was surrounded by more beggars. Soon people started gathering to watch the three of us walking. They took out their phones and clicked our pictures without our permission. James didn't care, he kept walking and Aeram and I followed him. Then he stopped at a spot and showed us a lone fishing boat. The tide was coming in and the sea was getting rough. The waves were slamming into the boat's loose side and there was a risk of it overturning and breaking on the jagged rocks below. James looked at the two of us and asked, "Will you keep the boat moored right there and let the waves smash it onto the rocks or will you set the boat free and let it find its own course whatever it may be?"

The question wasn't about the boat. I bit my lip. We stood there in silence. All three of us. A huge wave keeled the boat over onto the rocks. We heard a crack. It lay in two pieces on the jagged rocks, one side still tethered. Another wave broke onto the loose piece.

Aeram's eyes were red. He shouted, "I am not going to let her go, James. I need her to survive."

James put his elbows on both Aeram's shoulders and cradled his head in his hands. He said, "Then you'll break her into pieces. Do you want that?"

Aeram took his brother's hands in his and turned his head towards me. His nose was red and his lips were quivering. He was holding James's hands tight. My cheeks were wet with tears.

James watched me and spoke calmly into his ear, "I can't see her cry, Aeram. And neither can you. Let her go. For once, let her do what she wants to do for herself, not for you. Please."

A tear rolled down Aeram's cheek. "Saysha, I cannot live without you."

Before I could say anything, James did. He cupped Aeram's face in his palms again and said, "You don't have to live without her. She is still going to be family."

Aeram took James's hands in his and shook his head. He was crying. "Saysha, I know I am incapable of loving you the way he loves you and I am all messed up in my head but if you go… I promise I'll see a psychiatrist but please…"

He then grabbed James and buried his head in his shoulder and cried. James stroked his head. A crowd had gathered to watch the drama. Someone had spread the word and a few photographers had turned up. They were moving in on us.

The brothers remained oblivious to the change. James caressed Aeram's cheek and told him softly, "We both love you a lot, darling. Nobody is going to leave you. But you know much better than me that this wasn't the marriage you wanted for the two of you. You never raised your sails to set out on the journey, sweetheart. The wind can take you only this far."

Aeram clung to James for a long time. The crowds were going crazy with their cameras. He was weeping. I couldn't watch anymore and turned towards the sea. Then I heard a whisper, "Ok, I'll let her go."

James kissed Aeram on his cheek and said, "That's my boy! I love you so much."

Aeram was still holding him tight. He looked at James and shouted, "And you better stop pretending you're gay. I've known that you're not since the day I punched you for kissing me."

James laughed. "Really? Why didn't you tell me earlier?"

Wiping his tears, Aeram shrugged and smiled.

I stepped towards the two of them. Aeram hugged me and kissed me on my cheek. "I love you, Saysha. Always will."

I told him, "I love you too, Aeram."

Aeram drove us home. James and I sat in the backseat of the car.

He whispered, "Happy, Saysha?"

I rested my head on his chest and nodded while holding his Cross in my hand.

Aeram looked in the mirror. Our eyes met. He blew me a kiss and looked away.

Aeram flew to Delhi the next day. Ostensibly, be told us he wanted to be with Sanam and break the news of our separation to her, personally. He was very hurt but tried not to show it. I sat on the patio wrapped in James's arms as we watched the waves. He nibbled at my ear and asked, "Why do you love me, Saysha?" I turned to him, thinking he was joking but he was dead serious. I smiled and kissed him. Then I changed the topic. "Why did you tell him so suddenly, James? I thought you might wait for a few weeks."

He kissed me on my forehead. "I was waiting for you to decide to leave him. The moment you decided, I knew we were good.

I wanted you to be ready to leave him. He would let you go only and only if you would allow yourself to leave."

"How did you know I was ready? I never told you."

He laughed. "I have never seen you not eat a cake that has been lying in front of you for a full ten minutes."

I blushed and covered my face with my palms.

My phone buzzed. It was a message from Aeram: I love you, Saysha. I can't live without you. I'll wait for you to love me again.

I didn't know what to make of it. James looked at me. "What is it?" I showed him the message.

He laughed, "That's my boy!"

My brow furrowed. James gave me a peck on the cheek and said, "Give him time, Saysha. He is in pain. I am glad he's not thinking of killing himself."

James whipped out his phone and sent a text to Aeram: We're going to Goa. Join us there.

I was skeptical. "Is that a good idea?"

James was going to say something but his phone beeped. It was Aeram's reply: See you in two days.

James chuckled. "He can't stay away from us."

PART 10
GOA

Chapter 44

I was lounging on one of the armchairs on the porch reading Paulo Coelho's *Veronika Decides to Die* when the brothers rode in through the driveway on the Bullet. They had gone to Panjim to meet with Manohar Uncle. Aeram gave me a glance and headed straight to his bedroom upstairs. He was still hurting. James lingered around me and watched him go. Then he kicked off his shoes, took off his t-shirt and squeezed himself into the armchair next to me and gave me a kiss. He rested his head on my chest and closed his eyes. I stroked his head. A few minutes later, Aeram came out smelling citrusy after a shower. He saw us and stood near the armchair awkwardly. James didn't stir. Then he pushed the other armchair and brought it next to us. James raised his head to see what his brother was up to. When the armchairs were almost touching, Aeram stretched himself out on his and turned on his side facing James.

"I am never going to leave your side, Saysha," he told me in a deep sexy voice which still gave me goosebumps.

James laughed and teased him, "Aeram, you're going nuts!"

I tugged at a handful of his hair.

He winced. "Ouch! Saysha, you're hurting me."

I warned him, "Don't tease him, James. I can't tolerate anyone teasing, Aeram."

Aeram leaned in to give me a peck on my cheek. Then he lay down on his armchair, his head at the same level as James.

Caressing his brother's cheek, James whispered, "That makes two of us, Saysha."

Aeram smiled. He then picked up the book that I had dropped on the floor and started reading it.

In the late afternoon, Aeram had a press conference scheduled at the Taj Hotel. James and I decided to skip it and instead walked around the Albuquerque orchard holding our hands. "I want to show you something," he told me in a conspiratorial tone.

We kept walking beyond the orchard into the woods along the river. Long shadows of trees danced all over his body. We reached the top of a small hillock, the outer edge of the estate. The sun hung low in the sky. James stopped suddenly and bent down to pick up a pinch of mud. He took my hand and put it in my palm. I wondered what he was up to. He rubbed the mud off my hand till I was left with tiny black sugar-like crystals. I had never seen anything like that before.

"Haematite," James said, "Iron ore."

His index finger pointed to the ridge that ran along the river. He said, "This is the largest deposit of iron ore on this side of the Mandovi. It starts from our plantation and goes all along these hills. Guess, who wants it now?"

I had no clue. He passed me a thick visiting card. It read: "Svetlana Lebedinsky, Vice President, Mergers and Acquisitions, Lebedinsky Mining Company Pvt Ltd., Moscow, Russia."

What the...

Then it struck me: Why the estate had to be saved from Danny and Father Patrick, why it wasn't just about the orchard, the villa, the trees or even Aeram's happiness that James wanted to fight against the church to get it. He wanted to save it from something bigger and more powerful than anything we had known, something that was closing in on us.

Acknowledgments

Without the inputs of my friend Joy Vijay Fernandes, who is an intrinsic part of Don Bosco in Vadodara, Gujarat, and who painstakingly explained to me the hierarchies of the Roman Catholic Church, the different jurisdictions and roles of bishops and archbishops, the administrative functions of various dioceses and churches, this book would not have been possible. He also helped me design the cover for *Gone Goa Gone*. Elton Pinto, Reagan Rasquinha, Jesuit professors at my alma mater, St Xavier's College in Mumbai, and Andrea Maganlal have, on different occasions, given me insights into Goan culture that I imbibed and used in this book. I thank Samarth, Krupa and Tanmay Kholkar who run the BLive Electric Bike Tours in Goa for organizing one for my husband, Rachit Mankad, through Divar Island so he could record his observations and relay them to me because I was caring for my two-year-old son and couldn't go myself. Valuable inputs about mining came from Rachit who has a mining equipment business in Australia. I was first introduced to geology by my professors at St Xavier's College in Mumbai. Members of the Senior Reading Raccoons group on Facebook helped me find resources about the Inquisition in Goa, specifically pointing to A K Priolkar's *The Terrible Tribunal for the East — The Goa Inquisition* (1961).

As a community correspondent for The Times Group in Mumbai, I had the privilege of interacting with people of many faiths and denominations of Christianity, Judaism, Islam, Hinduism, Sikhism and Zoroastrian and the opportunity to volunteer at the Indooroopilly Uniting Church in Brisbane, Australia, allowed me to understand different cultures under one roof.

My mother, Sujata Sarkar, has been my pillar of strength and has pushed me to try newer forms of writing and media. A voracious reader, she read and guided me through the drafts of all the three books of *The Goa Saga*. My husband's cousin, Drumi Mankad, patiently listened to my character-sketches and came up with photographic references from her many travels to Goa. When I started writing *The Goa Saga*, she was the reader I had in mind: young, well-read, well-travelled, someone who loves Goa and has been there many times but still has to immerse herself into its beautiful culture. References to art direction in films came from Karan Bhatt, my former student and independent filmmaker and Darshana Dave from the Indian Foundation for the Arts in Bengaluru (formerly, Bangalore).

I am also grateful to the Indian film and fashion fraternity in Mumbai for giving me access to their homes, archives, offices, boutiques and hearts during my decades of association with them as student and journalist.

About the author

Eisha Sarkar is a podcaster, journalist, editor, designer and educator based in Vadodara, Gujarat. She has worked at Infinito Group in Australia, The Times Group in Mumbai, The MS University of Baroda, Pax Populi, UNICEF and National Institute of Design in Ahmedabad. Her non-fiction articles have been published in *UNICEF's publications, India Guide*

Gujarat, Chicken Soup for the Soul, The Times of India, Mumbai Mirror, Economic Times, Youth Incorporated, Femina, Filmfare, Bombay Times on subjects of travel, film, education and health. She has been a part of two writing programs, The Dangerous Women Project at the University of Edinburgh, UK, and The International Writing Program at the University of Iowa, USA. Her poetry has been published in *EquiVerseSpace*, an anthology and *Throw Me A Word*, an eBook. Eisha produces and hosts three podcast channels, *The Write Creed, TidyBytes with Reagan and Eisha* and *Footloose by Shre and Eish*.

THE GOA SAGA

MAD

&

MOONLY

PART 1
MUMBAI/NEW YORK

Chapter 1

Aeram left for the US early morning. James and I saw him off at the airport. He hugged us both but did not want to let go of James. We would join him a week later.

James and I had considered moving out of Aeram's house but he refused. The requirement for divorce was that we should live separately for a year, since we had been married for only a year but Aeram was tied emotionally to James so we couldn't live separately. Nonetheless, we found a solution. We rented a flat in the same building for James and myself but never visited it. We stayed with Aeram. I moved into the guest bedroom that James used as his room and Aeram was just across the corridor.

We hadn't announced our separation to anyone, not even to Mom and Dad. We thought we should wait till we came back from the US. The press would have a field day. The superstar was single again.

Aeram kissed me on both my cheeks and whispered, "I love you, Saysha."

"I love you too, Aeram." I had never stopped loving him though I loved James much more and saw in him the life partner I desired for myself, someone down-to-earth, with whom I could be just myself and keep my self-worth intact. He hugged James again. "I am going to miss you." James tousled his hair and kissed him on the forehead. Few photographers pulled out their cameras to take the pictures. There had been a lot of speculation in the papers about Aeram's relationship with his gay stunt-double, especially after pictures of the three of us at the Haji Ali Sea Face had become viral. Aeram had clung to James in despair after agreeing to let me go in full view of the crowd there. Everyone who had a phone had taken a picture. There were memes and debates. Some said Aeram was bisexual. Others said we were a threesome. Zarine managed the press. We never talked to anyone about it. No one knew James was Aeram's brother.

We headed back to the apartment. James slid his hand under my denim shirt dress while driving. A knot started to form in my stomach. As soon as we reached home, he grabbed me and gave me a long kiss. Then he picked me up and put me down on the twelve-seater dining table. We made love there. When Aeram was around, we had to curtail all our PDA. James had lived through a year of watching Aeram and me making out in front of him and he was adamant that Aeram should not be subjected to that pain. We had deliberately deferred our trip to the US by a week so we could have some time just for ourselves.

I woke up in the morning in James's room. Sunlight streaked his gorgeous face. I ran my tongue down his torso. He turned over and gave me sex. After we were done, he whispered, "Coffee?"

"Please," I said.

He got out of the bed to go to the kitchen. Then he stopped near the door, turned around and ordered, "Don't shower. You'll shower with me."

As we sat on the sofas on the patio sipping our coffees and watching the waves, I asked James about Tatiana's original letters. He still hadn't returned them to me. His jaw tightened. He stroked my hair and said, "Saysha, two of those letters are fake. Only one is original."

What? Why should Svetlana give me fake letters from my mother in Russian, a language I couldn't read?

"They weren't for you, Saysha," James said, reading my mind.

I was surprised. "Who were they for, then?"

"The one person in your vicinity who knows how to read Russian," he said and pointed a thumb to his chest, "Me."

Why did Svetlana give me letters that James should read? Maybe because she had assumed James was my boyfriend. But how did she know that he knew Russian?

James stroked my forehead. "My poor darling, don't stress so much. She probably thought you'll ask me to translate them for you. But you never even told me about them. Anyway, I can't tell you any more than I have already." He kissed me, took my hand in his and said, "Come, let's take a shower."

Chapter 2

Art director, Shweta Raisinghani's entire staff were camping at a farmhouse in Karjat for the whole month to build the sets for the period film *Darbaar*. While the art director had politely asked me to join, she hoped I would decline the invitation. She wanted to avoid the press and get work done. Since James had taken down Archbishop Patrick and Aeram's very public breakdown at Haji Ali, Shweta saw me as a liability. She preferred that I work from home because the office staff were always looking for gossip about my husband and his supposedly gay boyfriend. When I told her that I would be joining Aeram for most of his US schedule, she was more relieved than annoyed. I felt bad but James cheered me up by talking about the places we could visit. He also suggested that I could start looking for courses to study at a university abroad. It would widen my perspective of the world and help me find my feet again.

I was mulling over it when my phone buzzed. It was Rachel. She wanted to meet for a coffee again. I had avoided her after James had broken the news of Cyrus cheating on her with Tripti only to get back at her for teasing me. Aeram wouldn't have done that. He would have simply whisked me away. That was the biggest difference between the two. Aeram usually talked about hurting people but he had not even beaten up

Aakash at the masquerade ball when he had pulled me to dance with him. James had beaten anyone who had tried to grope me or touch me without my permission. He also seemed to be the more scheming and vindictive of the two. Nobody messed with James.

"Ok," I texted Rachel, as James walked in. Ever since he had told me that he worked for Interpol and Aeram had told him that he knew he wasn't gay, James had started dressing himself in casual suits. His tanned body looked stunning in beige. He ran his lips from my shoulder to the nape of my neck sending a shiver down my spine. I threw my head back to kiss him as he hugged me.

I whispered, "I'm going to meet Rachel. Want to come?"

He nibbled my earlobe and said, "Do you want me to?" He knew I was angry with him about what he had done the previous time we had met Rachel.

"Come."

He gave me a peck on my cheek and said, "Ok."

I texted Rachel: James will be joining us.

She replied: Fabulous!

We went down to the parking lot of the building but he didn't walk towards our car. He was busy on his phone. Without looking at me, he said, "We're Uber-ing."

Why? We had the Audi, the BMW and the Hyundai sitting in their parking lots.

He read my mind and smiled. "Because I want to have a make-out session and I can't if I am driving."

I blushed. He wrapped me in his arms and kissed me on my forehead. "Come on, the car's here."

Rachel saw us and got up from the table to greet us with a wide smile and big hugs. She took in James's new look and said in her flirty singsong voice, "Wow! You look good in clothes as well."

James laughed and asked me, "What will you have?"

We decided which coffees we wanted and he left Rachel and me at the table to order them.

"He could be in Hollywood, if only he had half the ambition of his boss."

I suppressed my laugh.

James brought our coffees; a double espresso for him, cappuccinos for Rachel and me and walnut brownies.

"When are you guys leaving for the US?" Rachel started the conversation.

"Next week," James answered without looking up from his coffee.

"Wow, James, you managed to have her all for yourself this week," Rachel quipped.

James grinned. I bit my lip.

He entwined his fingers in mine and kissed my hand. Then he told Rachel coolly, "She's mine. All mine. Just mine."

Rachel was shocked. Then, before she could ask him anything else, he chugged his coffee, picked up his phone and excused himself. "Give me a call, Saysha, once you're done and I'll come to pick you up in the Audi."

I could hear my heartbeats. Rachel collected herself and finally asked the question I was dreading.

"Are you cheating on Aeram?"

I sighed. "No."

"Then, what the hell did he just say?" She demanded an answer.

I had to tell the truth to someone for I couldn't hold it within me any longer. "Aeram and I are getting a divorce. But nobody knows about it, Rachel, so please don't tell anyone," I pleaded, keeping my voice as low as possible.

"What?" She gasped.

I nodded. My lips were quivering.

She put her hand on mine. "Saysha, I am so sorry."

I felt like opening up to her. She was one of my oldest friends. "I think we made a mistake rushing into it. You know, we had barely been together for just about three months over a period of three-and-a-half years. I wish we had given ourselves more time to understand what we both wanted from marriage."

"Oh darling." She hugged me. Then she asked, "So have you moved in with him?"

I shook my head.

"Then?"

"We still live with Aeram. He can't live without either of us."

"Are you insane?"

I laughed. "Aeram certainly is."

She smiled. "He is a nutcase. But seriously, why? How does this work? You both and him under the same roof. Three's a crowd, Saysha!"

I couldn't tell her James was Aeram's brother. "They are very close, Rachel, closer than I am to either of them."

She looked at me incredulously, "So the reports are true? They are a thing."

I laughed. "Rachel, neither of them is gay?"

She was shocked. "What? James is not gay?"

I shook my head. "No."

"Then why does he behave like one? Or actually he doesn't behave gay but is known to be gay."

I smiled. "There were rumours someone spread and he never bothered to correct them." I was proud of making that up.

"They've been the best of friends since childhood," I elaborated, "they cannot live without each other."

"Wow! Some friendship, Saysha. And look at us, we've been together since we were toddlers and I still have to text you to have coffee with me once a month."

I smiled and put a spoonful of walnut brownie into my mouth. It melted on my tongue.

Rachel watched me enjoy the brownie and asked, "After your divorce comes through, do you think Aeram might want to date me?"

What! I collected myself and brusquely told her, "Maybe you'll have to wait for over a year."

She noticed my discomfort and was pleased. "But seriously, Saysha, I think James is a better match for you. He's older, wiser and poorer," she opined.

I laughed. "Not too poor."

"Oh yes, the gift from Aeram. The most expensive thing a best friend had gifted me was a bag. I wish someone would give me a villa," she said and rolled her eyes. "Anyways, Saysha, I have to go now. There's a party at the Taj tonight so we have to get the cakes going. It was nice catching up with you and him. Love you, bye." She hugged me and left.

I called James who walked in through the door within a minute.

"You were here all along?"

He nodded.

"Then why did you leave?"

"I wanted you to tell her. You need to start telling people, Saysha, about your separation, at least to your loved ones. It will help you move on. Don't worry about his celebrity status, the press or the PR. They don't matter in the long run. You can only be free if you allow yourself to be." He kissed me on my forehead and we left in another Uber.

TO BE CONTINUED